Anonymous

# Reports of the Executive Committee and Treasurer of the New York Bridge Company

Anatiposi

Anonymous

# Reports of the Executive Committee and Treasurer of the New York Bridge Company

Reprint of the original, first published in 1872.

1st Edition 2023   |   ISBN: 978-3-38214-664-1

Anatiposi Verlag is an imprint of Outlook Verlagsgesellschaft mbH.

Verlag (Publisher): Outlook Verlag GmbH, Zeilweg 44, 60439 Frankfurt, Deutschland
Vertretungsberechtigt (Authorized to represent): E. Roepke, Zeilweg 44, 60439 Frankfurt, Deutschland
Druck (Print): Books on Demand GmbH, In de Tarpen 42, 22848 Norderstedt, Deutschland

| | | | |
|---|---|---|---:|
| | Brought forward | | $234,147 46 |
| Sept. 11.—Bodwell, Webster & Co | | | 400 00 |
| " 12. | " | | 562 62 |
| " 14. | " | | 592 50 |
| " 15. | " | | 652 75 |
| | " | | 268 00 |
| " 16. | " | | 311 29 |
| " 18. | " | | 298 28 |
| " 21. | " | | 424 14 |
| Oct. 2. | " | | 360 00 |
| | " | | 472 00 |
| | " | | 464 63 |
| " 4. | " | | 443 00 |
| " 5. | " | | 695 20 |
| " 6. | " | | 493 50 |
| | " | | 238 38 |
| " 7. | " | | 462 63 |
| " 9. | " | | 1,600 00 |
| | " | | 28,032 38 |
| | " | | 314 28 |
| | " | | 350 88 |
| " 10. | " | | 380 00 |
| " 16. | " | | 540 12 |
| " 17. | " | | 297 50 |
| " 24. | " | | 300 00 |
| | " | | 340 12 |
| " 28. | " | | 428 00 |
| Nov. 6. | " | | 9,456 24 |
| " 8. | " | | 1,012 43 |
| " 9. | " | | 1,586 11 |
| " 10. | " | | 371 71 |
| " 13. | " | | 991 00 |
| | " | | 10,000 00 |
| " 14. | " | | 538 71 |
| " 15. | " | | 300 00 |
| " 16. | " | | 643 29 |
| " 17. | " | | 670 71 |
| " 18. | " | | 313 28 |
| " 21. | " | | 527 30 |
| " 23. | " | | 743 57 |
| " 24. | " | | 576 60 |
| " 25. | " | | 392 00 |
| " 27. | " | | 288 80 |
| " 28. | " | | 598 00 |
| " 29. | " | | 528 57 |
| Dec. 1. | " | | 808 55 |
| " 4. | " | | 32,308 83 |
| " 8. | " | | 450 00 |
| " 29. | " | | 413 28 |
| 1872. | | | |
| Jan. 3. | " | | 438 00 |
| | Carried forward | | $337,826 64 |

# REPORTS

OF THE

# EXECUTIVE COMMITTEE,

AND

# TREASURER

OF THE

# NEW YORK BRIDGE COMPANY.

BROOKLYN:
EAGLE PRINT, 34 AND 36 FULTON STREET.

1872.

# REPORTS

OF THE

# EXECUTIVE COMMITTEE

AND

# TREASURER

OF THE

# NEW YORK BRIDGE COMPANY.

BROOKLYN:
EAGLE PRINT, 34 AND 36 FULTON STREET.

1872.

# REPORTS

## EXECUTIVE COMMITTEE AND TREASURER

OF THE

# NEW YORK BRIDGE COMPANY,

## 1872.

The Executive Committee respectfully present their
Annual Report:

Under the authority conferred upon them by resolu-
tion of the Board, they have continued with the construction of the bridge for the past year as rapidly as cir-
cumstances permitted. The Tower on the Brooklyn
side has been carried up to an elevation of 100 feet
above high water, and is progressing steadily upward.
The foundation of the Tower on the New York side of
the river has been sunk to its final depth of about 80
feet, and is so far advanced that in the course of a
month more it will, if no accidents intervene to prevent
it, be filled in and finished to above high water mark.
For the history and progress of the work during the year,
they refer with great satisfaction to the report of the
Chief Engineer, W. A. Roebling, Esq., now presented.
For the financial condition of the Company they refer
to the statements hereto appended, showing the receipts and expenditures of the Company in detail from

the commencement of the work to the first of May, 1872, viz :

(A.) Treasurer's statement of receipts and expenditures.

(B.) A statement of the receipts, showing from what persons and sources they have been received.

(C.) A statement of the expenditures, showing to whom and for what purposes they were made.

The report of the Superintendent shows the operations on the work, and is also now presented.

> S. L. HUSTED,
> J. S. T. STRANAHAN,
> HENRY W. SLOCUM,
> HENRY C. MURPHY, *ex off.*,

June 3, 1872.                                    *Committee.*

# A.

STATEMENT OF THE RECEIPTS AND EXPENDITURES OF THE NEW
YORK BRIDGE COMPANY TO AND INCLUDING APRIL 30, 1872.

## RECEIPTS.

| | |
|---|---:|
| Capital stock paid in | $2,762,400 00 |
| Rent | 4,560 00 |
| Material sold | 2,754 85 |
| Interest on deposits | 30,321 70 |
| Wharfage at Pier 29 | 3,587 71 |
| On sale of New York city bonds | 120,000 00 |
| Total | $2,923,624 26 |

## EXPENDITURES.

| | |
|---|---:|
| Engineering | $126,009 26 |
| Rent | 20,808 33 |
| Office expenses | 23,001 22 |
| Timber and lumber | 332,564 10 |
| Construction | 722,891 70 |
| Contingent expenses | 10,159 79 |
| Tools | 13,634 18 |
| Labor | 369,062 76 |
| Machinery | 108,154 19 |
| Freight, cartage, and towage | 9,617 06 |
| Printing and advertising | 1,092 51 |
| Land, land damages and buildings | 332,673 65 |
| Limestone | 171,277 09 |
| Insurance | 1,441 87 |
| Scows | 27,940 57 |
| Interest | 1,998 89 |
| Horses, wagons, and harness | 1,762 18 |
| Granite | 371,957 44 |
| Taxes | 3,772 76 |
| Office furniture | 5,337 23 |
| Bonds of the city of New York | 248,000 00 |
| Bodwell, Webster & Co., freight on account | 2,232 71 |
| Total | $2,905,389 49 |

| | |
|---|---:|
| Total receipts | $2,923,624 26 |
| Total expenditures | 2,905,389 49 |
| Balance of cash account | $18,234 77 |

Cash in Brooklyn Trust Co ........................ $1,672 05
" " Atlantic National Bank.................... 14,028 56
" " Long Island Bank........................ 1,610 14
Petty cash on hand............................. 924 02

Total....................................... $18,234 77

JOHN H. PRENTICE,

*Treasurer.*

BROOKLYN, May 1, 1872.

## B.

STATEMENT OF THE RECEIPTS OF THE NEW YORK BRIDGE COMPANY.
FROM ITS ORGANIZATION TO MAY 1, 1872.

CAPITAL STOCK PAID IN.

| Purchaser. | Shares. | Paid. | | |
|---|---|---|---|---|
| Henry C. Murphy.. | 250 | 60 per ct. | $15,000 00 | |
| Isaac Van Anden.. | 250 | 60 " | 15,000 00 | |
| William Marshall.. | 50 | 60 " | 3,000 00 | |
| Seymour L. Husted | 500 | 60 " | 30,000 00 | |
| Samuel McLean... | 50 | 40 " | 2,000 00 | |
| Arthur W. Benson. | 20 | 60 " | 1,200 00 | |
| Alexander McCue. | 250 | 60 " | 15,000 00 | |
| William M. Tweed | 420 | 40 " | 16,800 00 | |
| Peter B. Sweeny... | 420 | 40 " | 16,800 00 | |
| Hugh Smith...... | 420 | 40 " | 16,800 00 | |
| R. B. Connolly.... | 420 | 40 " | 16,800 00 | |
| Henry W. Slocum. | 250 | 60 " | 15,000 00 | |
| Jas. S. T. Stranahan | 500 | 60 " | 30,000 00 | |
| Kingsley & Keeney | 930 | 60 " | 55,800 00 | |
| John H. Prentice.. | 50 | 60 " | 3,000 00 | |
| Demas Barnes..... | 100 | 60 " | 6,000 00 | |
| John W. Lewis... | 50 | 60 " | 3,000 00 | |
| William Hunter, Jr. | 50 | 40 " | 2,000 00 | |
| Charles C. Martin . | 20 | 60 " | 1,200 00 | |
| City of New York. | 15,000 | .... | 698,000 00 | |
| City of Brooklyn.. | 30,000 | 60 " | 1,800,000 00 | |
| | | | | $2,762,400 00 |
| | 50,000 | | | |

Brought forward...................... $2,762,400 00

### RENTS.

| | | |
|---|---|---|
| 1871, Nov. 1.—W. H. Marston..... | $2,275 00 | |
| 1872, Feb. 1.— " " ..... | 2,275 00 | |
| " " 28.—David White...... | 10 00 | |
| | | 4,560 00 |

### MATERIAL SOLD.

| | | |
|---|---|---|
| A. T. Briggs, cement barrels.. | $988 51 | |
| Morton & Canda, " " .. | 61 50 | |
| Citizens' Gas-Light Co., " " .. | 41 23 | |
| H. A. Richardson, " " .. | 37 70 | |
| Page, Kidder & Fletcher, " .. | 99 40 | |
| Union Chemical Works, " " .. | 8 60 | |
| Captain of canal boat et al., " .. | 101 00 | |
| Union Chemical Works, tar barrels... | 63 70 | |
| James Binns, old iron...... | 20 16 | |
| D. W. Richards & Co., " ...... | 378 60 | |
| James Cumings, mud bucket.......... | 400 00 | |
| John Roach & Son, castings........ | 66 88 | |
| Received for pile-driver hammer...... | 12 00 | |
| Kingsley & Keeney, brick........... | 18 32 | |
| " " rubber boots.... | 49 93 | |
| T. C. Murray, gas cylinders.......... | 100 00 | |
| Noone & Madden, spruce spars....... | 18 00 | |
| C. N. Flanders, oil barrels........... | 3 50 | |
| A. Inslee, " ........... | 8 00 | |
| I. E. White, rope, etc............... | 46 56 | |
| For gas, old junk, candles, old fence, oil cans........................ | 231 26 | |
| | | 2,754 85 |

### INTEREST.

| | | |
|---|---|---|
| Brooklyn Trust Company, on deposits. | $18,038 20 | |
| Atlantic National Bank, " .. | 12,283 50 | |
| | | 30,321 70 |

### WHARFAGE.

Received from sundry vessels at Pier 29............ 3,587 71

Received on sales of N. Y. City Bonds............. 120,000 00

Total........................... $2,923,624 26

# C.

STATEMENT OF THE EXPENDITURES OF THE NEW YORK BRIDGE
COMPANY, FROM ITS ORGANIZATION TO MAY 1, 1872.

### No. 1.—ENGINEERING.

Salaries, instruments, drawing materials, models,
surveying, boring, etc........................... $126,009 26

### No. 2.—RENTS.

Offices, stone yard, and Water street, New York.... 20,808 33

### No. 3.—OFFICE EXPENSES.

Salaries, stationery, books, and miscellaneous items.. 23,001 22

### No. 4.—TIMBER AND LUMBER.

| | | |
|---|---|---|
| T. M. Mayhew & Co.................. | $46,915 56 | |
| "      "      "      .................. | 14.588 98 | |
| M. A. Wilder, Son & Co............... | 80,633 53 | |
| Snow & Richardson .................. | 850 22 | |
| New York and Brooklyn Saw Mill and Lumber Company.................. | 34,686 81 | |
| H. N. Conklin, Son & Beers........... | 17,463 32 | |
| Jonathan Beers...................... | 29,683 97 | |
| George R. Alexander................. | 500 89 | |
| P. M. McGovern, storage............. | 2,513 24 | |
| J. F. Phelps, Jr., & Co., storage........ | 212 58 | |
| Phelps & Kimpland.................. | 17,495 68 | |
| D. A. Youngs...................... | 29 75 | |
| W. H. Dunn....................... | 2,867 04 | |
| A. Ammerman...................... | 84.122 53 | |
| | | 332,564 10 |

### No. 5.—CONTINGENT EXPENSES.

Funeral expenses, traveling expenses, legal expenses,
donations to widows, medical services, collations at
launching of caissons, tow boats at launching and
towing caisson, expenses visiting stone quarries, etc.  10,159 79

### No. 6.

Tools............................................ 13,634 18

### No. 7.

Labor ........................................... 369,062 76

### No. 8.

Machinery ...................................... 108.154 19

Carried forward........................ $1,003.393 83

Brought forward........................ $1,003,393 83

### No. 9.

Freight, cartage, and towage.................... 9,617 06

### No. 10.

Printing and advertising........................ 1,092 51

### No. 11.

Land, land damages, and buildings .............. 332,673 65

### No. 12.—LIMESTONE.

| | | |
|---|---|---|
| Noone & Company................... | $112,109 17 | |
| Read & Morrell.................... | 19,139 17 | |
| Lake Champlain Blue-stone Company .. | 40,028 75 | |
| | | 171,277 09 |

### No. 13.

Insurance...................................... 1,441 87

Taxes ......................................... 3,772 76

### No. 14.—SCOWS.

| | | |
|---|---|---|
| New York and Brooklyn Saw Mill and Lumber Company.................. | $15,800 00 | |
| A. Ammerman...................... | 8,800 00 | |
| Atlantic Dock Company.............. | 2,500 00 | |
| D. Burtis, Jr., for repairs ............ | 802 67 | |
| Sundry materials for repairs.......... | 37 90 | |
| | | 27,940 57 |

### No. 15.

Interest ...................................... 1,998 89

### No. 16.

Horses, wagons, and harness .................... 1,762 18

### No. 17.—GRANITE.

| | | |
|---|---|---|
| Bodwell, Webster & Co............... | $371,345 62 | |
| C. P. Dixon........................ | 611 82 | |
| | | 371,957 44 |

### No. 18.

Office furniture ............................... 5,337 23

### No. 19.

Bonds of the City of New York................... 248,000 00

Bodwell, Webster, & Co., freights paid on their account....................................... 2,232 71

Carried forward...................... ..... $2,182,497 79

Brought forward ........................ $2,182,497 79

No. 20.—CONSTRUCTION ACCOUNT.

| | | |
|---|---:|---:|
| Webb & Bell, building caissons, and material........................ | $213,020 42 | |
| John Roach & Son, iron-work for caissons...:..................... | 54,208 37 | |
| Hubbard & Whittaker, iron-work for caisson, etc .............. | 19,488 85 | |
| Divine Burtis, Jr., work and material on caisson...................... | 71,391 48 | |
| Marston & Powers, coal and labor.... | 16,601 53 | |
| Mason & Watts, gravel and sand..... | 24,841 70 | |
| R. S. Place & Co., iron-work........ | 9,127 02 | |
| Egleston Bros. & Co., iron and steel.. | 7,823 30 | |
| James O. Morse, iron pipes, fittings, etc | 9,605 79 | |
| Sanderson, Bros. & Co., steel........ | 750 34 | |
| Aymar, De Grauw & Co., and De Grauw, Aymar & Co., rope, waste, packing, chains, oakum, etc. .............. | 12,377 08 | |
| John A. Roebling's Sons, wire rope, sockets, etc...................... | 5,825 98 | |
| Burr & Co., blocks, sheaves, etc.... . | 2,013 50 | |
| F. O. Norton, cement ............... | 24,225 35 | |
| Morton, Canda & Co., and John Morton & Son, cement, lime and brick. | 25,632 36 | |
| A. B. Stearns & Co., coal.......... | 5,958 86 | |
| J. B. Carr & Co., chains........... | 313 88 | |
| Abraham Inslee, iron-work......... | 1,843 36 | |
| A. Gross & Co., candles............ | 4,399 30 | |
| Jas. W. Valentine, cement and coal.. | 172 50 | |
| Sears, Leavitt & Co., ropes, chains, nails, spikes, etc.................. | 2,169 27 | |
| Richardson, Boynton & Co., steel, stoves and fixtures.............. | 172 58 | |
| N. Y. Belting and Packing Co., hose, belting, etc...................... | 1,599 35 | |
| Brooklyn Gas-Light Co., gas........ | 963 35 | |
| Holden, Hopkins & Stokes, iron..... | 356 89 | |
| Coplay Cement Co., cement........ | 2,642 50 | |
| Combination Rubber Co., hose, packing, belting, couplings, etc........ | 1,398 93 | |
| Pool & Bergen, and Geo. Pool & Sons, paints, oil, lanterns, lamps, etc..... | 1,001 12 | |
| John Bunce, hardware.............. | 651 42 | |
| Jos. H. Mumby, horse feed......... | 469 45 | |
| Wm. Taylor & Sons, iron-work..... | 678 86 | |
| N. Y. Oxygen Gas Co., oxygen gas... | 4,682 54 | |
| Jas. McFarlan, Jr., iron-work....... | 472 55 | |
| Hazard Powder Co., powder........ | 2,536 00 | |
| I. E. White, piles, labor, and use of pile-driver ...................... | 1,647 65 | |

Carried forward................$531,063 43 $2,182,497 79

| | | |
|---|---|---|
| Brought forward................ | $531,063 43 | $2,182,497 79 |
| Abbott & Co., gravel roofing and cementing boilers.................. | 243 65 | |
| B. T. Benton, iron pipes, fittings, etc. | 1,629 31 | |
| Davis & Riker, pipe and fittings, packing, spikes, etc.................. | 99 09 | |
| John Frazier, powder cans, tin-work, etc............................ | 482 34 | |
| Laflin & Rand Powder Co., powder... | 45 00 | |
| Holton & Gray, and Holton & Dickinson, rubber springs, gaskets, washers, etc ........................ | 668 25 | |
| Henry Elliott & Co., and Wallace & Elliott, rubber boots............. | 2,388 25 | |
| Powell M'fg Co., and R. I. Powell, powder cans, tin-work, etc........ | 381 95 | |
| Cuthbert & Cunningham, coal tar.... | 17 75 | |
| W. C. Kingsley, superintendence..... | 125,000 00 | |
| C. & R. Poillon, spars.............. | 167 50 | |
| S. S. Goodwin, earth filling......... | 82 00 | |
| W. S. Tisdale & Co., nails and spikes. | 460 85 | |
| Miscellaneous items from petty cash.. | 1,416 55 | |
| *Miscellaneous Items—* | | |
| India Rubber Roofing Co., roofing.... | 149 07 | |
| John McRoberts, gravel and sand.... | 171 35 | |
| R. J. Hutchinson, powder cans....... | 75 00 | |
| P. Bracken, stone and sand......... | 72 00 | |
| J. A. Bouker, stone................. | 486 28 | |
| J. S. Turner, water................. | 239 95 | |
| John J. Wilson, cement............. | 214 00 | |
| W. M. Tebo, use of steam tug ...... | 1,562 50 | |
| F. Hobson & Son, steel............. | 200 55 | |
| John McGinn, services as pilot...... | 160 00 | |
| Wharfage of caissons.............. | 1,295 50 | |
| P. C. Shultz, towing caissons........ | 450 00 | |
| P. C. Coffin, spikes, nails, etc........ | 75 56 | |
| Wm. Dorian, rigging at caisson...... | 249 15 | |
| Vanpelt & Moore, rope, canvas, oil clothing, etc...................... | 971 88 | |
| Armstrong & Blacklin, plumbing and gas-fitting..................... | 1,678 70 | |
| J. T. Martin, inspector of dredging... | 234 00 | |
| C. N. Flanders, oil................. | 1,070 84 | |
| Brien, Adams & Brien, plumbing, gas-fixtures, etc..................... | 272 87 | |
| American Tool Steel Co., steel....... | 490 55 | |
| G. R. Alexander, hardwood lumber.. | 108 92 | |
| A. M. C. Smith, belting, hose, etc ... | 162 46 | |
| Engel, Rothermel & Co., coal....... | 632 70 | |
| Richard Bracken, stone............. | 66 50 | |
| G. L. Enggren, boring at Pier 29..... | 950 01 | |
| Carried forward............ | $676,186 26 | $2,182,497 79 |

| | | |
|---|---|---|
| Brought forward............ | $676,186 26 | $2,182,497 79 |
| Caffrey & Wilson, testing cylinders, | | |
| hydrogen gas.................. | 153 82 | |
| John Voorhies, stone.............. | 96 25 | |
| Geo. Carr & Co., felting boilers...... | 249 00 | |
| P. W. Shute, broken slate........... | 12 00 | |
| Union, Ackron, Cement Co., cement.. | 37 00 | |
| S. T. Baker & Co., oil.............. | 227 68 | |
| R. Dudgeon, repairing jacks........ | 48 50 | |
| J. J. Reimer & Co., woodenware..... | 86 03 | |
| M. McKenney, iron-work........... | 177 20 | |
| Smith & Hall, rollers, wedges, etc.... | 243 50 | |
| Chapman Slate Co., broken slate..... | 90 50 | |
| Phelps & Kimpland, piles, towing, etc | 1,109 26 | |
| Bangs & Gaynor, cement........... | 290 40 | |
| G. W. Gallaway, oil............... | 98 25 | |
| C. H. Delamater, iron-work;........ | 282 86 | |
| H. A. Rogers & Co., felting boilers, | | |
| belting, etc..................... | 202 00 | |
| D. Fithian, window sashes, etc....... | 179 90 | |
| W. C. Wright & Co., oil............ | 157 95 | |
| F. W. Devoe, oil................. | 415 82 | |
| Joseph Nason & Co., pipes and fittings | 411 52 | |
| Jas. Cumings, iron-work, blocks, etc.. | 202 25 | |
| W. E. Woodruff, painting.......... | 651 55 | |
| Salamander Grate Bar Co., grate bars. | 351 94 | |
| Washington Iron Works, iron-work... | 129 11 | |
| Livingston & Cheritree Manufacturing | | |
| Co., hardware.................. | 14 98 | |
| David Dows & Co., storage of cement. | 378 43 | |
| Page, Kidder & Fletcher, tar and pitch. | 97 50 | |
| Buell & Co., roofing............... | 584 66 | |
| N. Y. Creosoting Works, creosoting | | |
| plank........................ | 1,106 88 | |
| W. H. Rushmore, cement........... | 100 00 | |
| A. H. Acken, traveling expenses..... | 135 21 | |
| Mason & Martin, repairing boilers.... | 250 13 | |
| Wm. Cochrane, labor as rigger....... | 113 17 | |
| Union Chemical Works, tar, pitch, and | | |
| felt ......................... | 446 49 | |
| Del. & Hudson Canal Co., coal...... | 212 50 | |
| John Marx, galvanizing iron........ | 159 60 | |
| T. J. Meadon, tinning on caisson..... | 108 50 | |
| John Gray & Co., woodenware....... | 138 25 | |
| A. C. Keeney, sand................ | 615 39 | |
| W. A. Freeborn & Co., asphalt, tar, etc. | 99 88 | |
| Union White Lead Co., lead and oil.. | 124 75 | |
| Keeping of one horse used by Super- | | |
| intendent, 15 months............ | 375 00 | |
| John Burt, diving at Pier 29 ........ | 150 00 | |
| Nicholas Kane, chain, canvas, ham- | | |
| mocks, etc.................... | 136 17 | |
| Carried forward............... | $687,438 04 | $2,182,497 79 |

| | | |
|---|---:|---:|
| Brought forward.............. | $687,438 04 | $2,182,497 79 |
| Morris & Cumings, excavating at Pier 29............................... | 9,000 00 | |
| Morris & Cumings, removing stone from river at R. H.................... | 250 00 | |
| Richardson, Meriam & Co., castings, straps, etc........................ | 65 03 | |
| W. D. Andrews & Bro., use of steam engine. etc........................ | 236 25 | |
| Cory & Co., oil.................... | 475 18 | |
| John Cochrane, agent, iron-work..... | 696 50 | |
| Pechell & Co., paint................ | 84 82 | |
| Wm. Butcher Steel Works, steel links and pins.......................... | 6,013 41 | |
| McMann & Russell, iron pipe and fittings............................. | 310 36 | |
| R. A. Chesebrough, oil........... | 121 12 | |
| S. S. Goodwin, earth filling ........ | 138 80 | |
| B. J. Drew, stoves and fixtures....... | 170 95 | |
| Asbestos Felting Co., covering boilers. | 924 15 | |
| T. & A. Walsh, dock stone.......... | 2,117 81 | |
| Theo. Smith & Bro., building dredge buckets, repairs, etc.............. | 1,355 78 | |
| Clark, Wilson & Co., hardware ...... | 34 26 | |
| Hess & Co., galvanizing iron ........ | 134 28 | |
| T. New, roofing..................... | 169 24 | |
| Leeds, Clark & Co., oiled clothing.... | 228 00 | |
| T. A. Scott, diving................. | 357 50 | |
| Goodyear Rubber Co., rubber boots... | 1,704 35 | |
| Pitkin & Co., bedding.............. | 67 80 | |
| A. Schrœder, cylinder bed plate, etc.. | 93 42 | |
| G. A. Merwin & Co., coffee.......... | 83 46 | |
| J. W. Kissam, cooking utensils, etc... | 36 10 | |
| West Va. Oil and O. Land Co., oil.... | 180 50 | |
| Morris, Tasker & Co., iron cocks..... | 140 00 | |
| M. Murphy, pilotage of caisson....... | 150 00 | |
| Wm. Porter & Sons, lamps, etc ...... | 105 47 | |
| Geo. T. Sutton & Co., sugar......... | 106 76 | |
| Building Material Co., cement....... | 2,100 00 | |
| N. Y. Gas-Light Co., gas........... | 1,223 38 | |
| Phelps, Dodge & Co., pig lead ...... | 3,713 21 | |
| Jas. Williamson & Co., pig iron...... | 1,150 00 | |
| Jas. O'Brien, stone................. | 335 00 | |
| Chas. McManus, gravel............. | 346 37 | |
| Phœnix Iron Co., eye bars and pins... | 156 42 | |
| W. H. Paine, material and labor at caisson........................ | 70 82 | |
| N. Morton, tar..................... | 24 00 | |
| A. K. Mescrole, coal, lime, and cement | 31 75 | |
| Tillotson & Co., blasting wire........ | 60 00 | |
| i. Woodbury, fuse................... | 66 00 | |
| One barrel cement.................. | 1 80 | |
| Carried forward.............. | $722,268 09 | $2,182,497 79 |

14

| | | |
|---|---:|---:|
| Brought forward............. | $722,268 09 | $2,182,497 79 |
| John Bowie. lead castings........... | 28 50 | |
| Lindsay, W. & Co., spikes, sponges, etc.................... | 66 14 | |
| Walton & Co., sponges............. | 9 82 | |
| F. H. Schneider & Co., cementing boilers.... .................... | 39 09 | |
| Mulford & Co., nails and spikes...... | 17 00 | |
| N. J. Car Spring Co., gaskets........ | 19 97 | |
| W. C. Bramhill & Co., belting, packing, etc...................... | 25 95 | |
| N. & H. O'Donnell, hogsheads....... | 61 09 | |
| Forge Co., canopy for forge........ | 14 50 | |
| Salamander Works, pipes and fittings. | 34 80 | |
| Chrome Steel Co., steel............. | 21 25 | |
| Eckford Iron Works, iron-work...... | 12 32 | |
| W. L. Holmes, horse feed.......... | 25 56 | |
| Henry Moore, oil cups, etc.......... | 44 00 | |
| James Goff, use of row-boats....... | 40 00 | |
| C. Donohue, horse-shoeing.......... | 42 37 | |
| R. I. Powell, tin-ware............. | 17 25 | |
| Rubber suit for Inspector........... | 15 00 | |
| Repairs to diving-bell............. | 8 00 | |
| E. K. Richards & Co.. ship timber.... | 12 00 | |
| Page. Thomas & Co., roofing........ | 40 23 | |
| A. M. Ingersoll, row-boat........... | 80 00 | |
| E. Daly, adm'x, repairing wagon...... | 15 00 | |
| James L. Moore, repairing harness, etc. | 27 44 | |
| Charles A. Willard, coal............ | 32 75 | |
| Ash & Buckbee, plumbing and gas-fitting.............................. | 37 38 | |
| H. A. White & Co.. oil ............ | 31 00 | |
| Matthew March, leather ........... | 11 36 | |
| Howard & Morse, wire-work ....... | 23 55 | |
| G. Tagliabue, glass tubes, etc....... | 10 20 | |
| Pearce & Mitchell, castings......... | 21 45 | |
| New York Lighterage Company, lightering pig iron.............. | 18 75 | |
| Martin J. Brien, plumbing......... | 20 13 | |
| | $723,191 76 | |

Less amount received from Wilder, Son & Co., for labor $219 25
Less discount from Egleston, Bros. & Co.............. 80 81

300 06

722,891 70

Total.................................................... $2,905,389 49

# DETAILED STATEMENT

OF THE

# EXPENDITURES

OF THE

# NEW YORK BRIDGE COMPANY,

FROM ITS ORGANIZATION TO MAY 1, 1872.

ENGINEERING.

1869.

| | | | |
|---|---|---|---|
| Aug. | 5.—W. J. McAlpine | $1,000 | 00 |
| | John J. Serrell | 1,000 | 00 |
| | Julius W. Adams | 1,000 | 00 |
| | James P. Kirkwood | 1,000 | 00 |
| | J. Dutton Steele | 1,000 | 00 |
| | Horatio Allen | 1,000 | 00 |
| | Benjamin H. Latrobe | 1,000 | 00 |
| " | 9.—Salaries for July | 498 | 48 |
| | Instruments, models, etc | 923 | 24 |
| | Contingent expenses | 135 | 23 |
| Sept. | 3.—Salaries for August | 916 | 45 |
| | Contingent expenses | 35 | 27 |
| Oct. | 25.—Salaries for September | 859 | 00 |
| | Instruments, etc | 112 | 54 |
| | Contingent expenses | 7 | 90 |
| Nov. | 3.—Salaries for October | 864 | 50 |
| | Contingent expenses | 17 | 41 |
| Nov. | 16.—Instruments and tools | 15 | 68 |
| " | 30.— " " | 8 | 30 |
| Dec. | 6.—Salary, H. Allen, to November 1, 1869 | 2,000 | 00 |

1870.

| | | | |
|---|---|---|---|
| Jan. | 17.—Surveying, boring for foundations, etc | 3,318 | 95 |

1869.

| | | | |
|---|---|---|---|
| Dec. | 6.—Salaries for November | 937 | 50 |
| " | 10.—Instruments | 8 | 60 |

1870.

| | | | |
|---|---|---|---|
| Jan. | 3.—Salaries for December, 1869 | 873 | 50 |
| " | 11.—Stationery and drawing materials | 52 | 00 |
| " | 31.—Salaries for January | 840 | 00 |
| | Salary W. A. Roebling, to July 22, 1869 | 3,250 | 00 |
| | Salary estate of John A. Roebling, to July 22, 1869 | 17,333 | 33 |
| | Stationery and drawing materials | 10 | 10 |
| Feb. | 7.—Salaries to February 1, 1870, Roebling, Allen, Martin | 7,416 | 66 |
| " | 8.—Expenses to Cincinnati and in Brooklyn of consulting engineers | 4,516 | 65 |
| Mar. | 7.—Salaries for February | 2,694 | 65 |
| " | 9.—Models, etc | 82 | 99 |
| April | 4.—Salaries for March, 1870 | 2,768 | 15 |
| " | 5.—Miscellaneous items | 16 | 75 |
| May | 2.—Salaries for April | 2,626 | 65 |
| June | 6.— " May | 2,704 | 65 |
| " | 9.—Miscellaneous items, by W. H. Paine | 39 | 15 |
| July | 5.—Salaries for June | 2,819 | 65 |
| Aug. | 9.— " July | 2,676 | 65 |
| Sept. | 6.— " August | 2,717 | 65 |

| | | | |
|---|---|---|---|
| | Carried forward | $71,198 | 23 |

| | | | |
|---|---|---|---:|
| | Brought forward........................ | $71,198 | 23 |
| Oct. | 3.—Salaries for September .................. | 2.727 | 15 |
| Nov. | 7.— " October .................... | 2,937 | 73 |
| " | 18.—Drawing material ...................... | 22 | 65 |
| Dec. | 5.—Salaries for November .................. | 2,916 | 60 |

1871.

| | | | |
|---|---|---|---:|
| Jan. | 3.—Salaries for December, 1870 ............. | 2,905 | 48 |
| Feb. | 6.— " January ..................... | 2,936 | 98 |
| Mar. | 6.— " February ..................... | 2,913 | 48 |
| April | 3.— " March ..................... | 2,946 | 48 |
| May | 1.— " April..................... | 2,952 | 48 |
| June | 5.— " May..................... | 2,935 | 98 |
| July | 10.— " June ..................... | 2,932 | 98 |
| " | 12.—Surveying at Pier 29 ..................... | 25 | 00 |
| Aug. | 7.—Salaries for July ..................... | 3,069 | 48 |
| Sept. | 8.— " August ..................... | 3,099 | 48 |
| Oct. | 9.— " September .................. | 2,710 | 66 |
| Nov. | 6.— " October..................... | 2,922 | 32 |
| " | 18.—C. C. Martin, salary for November, in part.. | 250 | 00 |
| " | 29.—D. S. Rhule, salary to November 11........ | 49 | 50 |
| Dec. | 4.—Salaries for November .................. | 2,394 | 82 |
| " | 29.—C. C. Martin, salary for December......... | 416 | 66 |

1872.

| | | | |
|---|---|---|---:|
| Jan. | 6.—Salaries for December, 1871 ............. | 2,433 | 66 |
| Feb. | 5.— " January ..................... | 2,812 | 82 |
| Mar. | 6.—W. H. Paine, on account of salary for | | |
| | February....................... | 100 | 00 |
| " | 11.—Salaries for February..................... | 2,699 | 32 |
| April | 8.— " March ..................... | 2,799 | 32 |

| | | |
|---|---|---:|
| Total...............................; | $126,009 | 26 |

1869. RENTS.

| | | | |
|---|---|---|---:|
| Oct. | 25.—Rent of offices to Aug. 1, 1869.......... | $537 | 50 |
| Nov. | 15.— " " Nov. 1, 1869.......... | 537 | 50 |

1870.

| | | | |
|---|---|---|---:|
| Feb. | 7.— " " Feb. 1, 1870.......... | 825 | 00 |
| " | 8.— " " May 1, 1869.......... | 358 | 33 |
| May | 2.— " " " 1870.......... | 825 | 00 |
| Aug. | 9.— " " Aug. 1.............. | 825 | 00 |
| " | 11.—Rent of stone yard, Atlantic Dock Co. to | | |
| | Aug. 1........................ | 1,250 | 00 |
| Nov. | 7.—Rent of offices to Nov. 1............... | 825 | 00 |
| " | 8.—Rent of stone yard to Nov. 1, Atlantic | | |
| | Dock Co...................... | 1,250 | 00 |
| Dec. | 5.—Rent of No. 284 Water street, N. Y., to | | |
| | Jan. 10, 1871................... | 200 | 00 |

| | | |
|---|---|---:|
| Carried forward....................... | $7,433 | 33 |

|  |  |  |
|---|---|---|
| Brought forward..................... | | $7,433 33 |

**1871.**

| Feb. | 6.—Rent of offices to Feb. 1............. | 825 00 |
|---|---|---|
| " | 13.—Rent of stone yard to Atlantic Dock Co. to Feb. 1.................. | 1,250 00 |
| May | 1.—Rent of stone yard to Atlantic Dock to May 1.................. | 1,250 00 |
|  | Rent of stone yard to S. S. & B. A. Haff.. | 750 00 |
|  | Rent of offices to May 1.............. | 825 00 |
| Aug. | 7.— " " Aug. 1.............. | 825 00 |
|  | Rent of stone yard to Atlantic Dock Co... | 1,250 00 |
|  | Rent of stone yard to S. S. & B. A. Haff... | 750 00 |
| Nov. | 6.—Rent of stone yard to S. S. & B. A. Haff to Nov. 1.......... | 750 00 |
|  | Rent of stone yard to Atlantic Dock Co., to Nov. 1.................. | 1,250 00 |
|  | Rent of offices to Nov. 1.............. | 825 00 |

**1872.**

| Feb. | 5.—Rent of offices to Feb. 1............ | 825 00 |
|---|---|---|
|  | Rent of stone yard to S. S. & B. A. Haff.. | 750 00 |
| " | 6.— " " to Atlantic Dock Co... | 1,250 00 |

| Total ..................... | | $20,808 33 |
|---|---|---|

### OFFICE EXPENSES.

**1869.**

| Nov. | 8.—R. M. Whiting, Jr., stationery, etc........ | $138 60 |
|---|---|---|
|  | Standard Press, stationery, printing, etc.... | 1,032 73 |
| " | 30.—P. M. Beam, salary to date.............. | 78 00 |
|  | Miscellaneous items................... | 72 17 |
| Dec. | 6.—O. P. Quintard, salary to December 1...... | 249 42 |
| " | 27.—Miscellaneous items.................. | 26 57 |

**1870.**

| Jan. | 3.—Salaries for December, 1869............. | 262 33 |
|---|---|---|
| " | 10.—R. M. Whiting. Jr., stationery, etc........ | 417 17 |
| " | 30.—Salaries for January................. | 260 33 |
|  | Miscellaneous items.................. | 37 97 |
| Mar. | 7.—Salaries for February................. | 256 33 |
| " | 14.—Miscellaneous items in February.......... | 26 59 |
| April | 4.—R. M. Whiting, Jr., stationery, etc........ | 77 30 |
|  | Salaries for March................. | 262 33 |
| " | 5.—Miscellaneous items in March........... | 31 56 |
| " | 6.—Brooklyn Eagle, books and stationery..... | 70 00 |
| May | 2.—Salaries for April................. | 260 33 |
| " | 5.—Miscellaneous items for April........... | 44 87 |
| " | 31.— " " May.............. | 119 99 |
| June | 6.—Salaries for May.............. | 208 33 |
|  | Brooklyn Eagle, books and stationery..... | 83 25 |
| " | 30.—Miscellaneous items in June............. | 60 61 |

| Carried forward ................. | | $4,076 78 |
|---|---|---|

| | | |
|---|---|---:|
| | Brought forward............................ | $4,076 78 |
| July | 5.—Salaries for June....................... | 401 33 |
| " | 29.—Hosford & Sons, stationery.............. | 40 39 |
| " | 30.—Miscellaneous items..................... | 74 07 |
| Aug. | 9.—Salaries for July....................... | 718 66 |
| " | 26.—Hosford & Sons, stationery.............. | 21 20 |
| " | 31.—Miscellaneous items..................... | 82 20 |
| Sept. | 6.—Salaries for August..................... | 720 66 |
| " | 7.—Brooklyn Eagle, stationery, etc........... | 59 25 |
| " | 10.—Benoit & Wood, drawing materials........ | 14 00 |
| " | 30.—Miscellaneous items..................... | 139 89 |
| Oct. | 3.—Salaries for September.................. | 718 66 |
| " | 7.—R. M. Whiting, Jr., stationery........... | 77 85 |
| " | 31.—Miscellaneous items..................... | 71 96 |
| Nov. | 7.—Salaries for October.................... | 718 66 |
| | Brooklyn Eagle, stationery.............. | 33 00 |
| " | 18.—Hosford & Sons, " ............... | 48 20 |
| " | 30.—Miscellaneous items..................... | 64 35 |
| Dec. | 5.—Salaries for November.................. | 718 66 |
| " | 6.—Brooklyn Eagle, stationery.............. | 31 20 |
| " | 31.—Miscellaneous items..................... | 79 95 |
| | 1871. | |
| Jan. | 3.—Salaries for December, 1870.............. | 720 66 |
| " | 31.—Miscellaneous items..................... | 54 14 |
| | J. H. Forker, salary to January 11........ | 44 35 |
| Feb. | 6.—Salaries for January.................... | 635 33 |
| " | 9.—R. M. Whiting, Jr., stationery........... | 29 05 |
| " | 17.—Hosford & Sons, " ........... | 27 65 |
| | Miscellaneous items.................... | 50 46 |
| March | 6.—Salaries for February.................... | 648 33 |
| " | 7.—Brooklyn Eagle, stationery, etc........... | 69 25 |
| " | 8.—Benoit & Wood, " ........... | 21 95 |
| " | 31.—Miscellaneous items..................... | 83 20 |
| April | 3.—Salaries for March..................... | 717 33 |
| " | 4.—Brooklyn Eagle, stationery, etc........... | 10 50 |
| " | 6.—Hosford & Sons, " ........... | 19 00 |
| " | 29.—Miscellaneous items..................... | 55 26 |
| May | 1.—Salaries for April..................... | 723 33 |
| " | 12.—Hosford & Sons, books, etc............... | 22 00 |
| " | 31.—Miscellaneous items..................... | 57 57 |
| June | 5.—Salaries for May....................... | 729 33 |
| " | 6.—Benoit & Wood, stationery....:........ | 30 30 |
| " | 13.—Brooklyn Eagle, books, etc............... | 21 25 |
| " | 30.—Miscellaneous items..................... | 106 65 |
| July | 10.—Salaries for June...................... | 726 33 |
| " | 14.—Benoit & Wood, stationery, etc........... | 31 35 |
| " | 19.—Hosford & Sons, " ........... | 66 45 |
| " | 31.—Miscellaneous items..................... | 92 10 |
| Aug. | 7.—Salaries for July ..................... | 726 33 |
| " | 10.—Hosford & Sons, stationery ............. | 20 85 |
| " | 31.—Miscellaneous items..................... | 61 58 |
| | Carried forward........................ | $15,512 80 |

| | | |
|---|---|---:|
| | Brought forward .......................... | $15,512 80 |
| Sept. | 8.—Salaries for August..................... | 773 33 |
| " | 30.—Miscellaneous items ................... | 131 56 |
| Oct. | 9.—Salaries for September.................. | 773 33 |
| " | 11.—Hosford & Sons, stationery ............ | 18 40 |
| " | 31.—Miscellaneous items ................... | 112 61 |
| Nov. | 6.—Salaries for October.................... | 773 33 |
| " | 29.—Miscellaneous items.................... | 109 93 |
| Dec. | 4.—Salaries for November................... | 773 33 |
| " | 11.—Brooklyn Eagle, books.................. | 27 00 |
| " | 30.—Miscellaneous items.................... | 69 96 |

1872.

| | | |
|---|---|---:|
| Jan. | 6.—Salaries for December, 1870............. | 773 33 |
| " | 12.—Benoit & Wood, drawing materials, etc ... | 58 35 |
| " | 18.—Hosford & Sons, stationery ............ | 81 87 |
| " | 31.—Miscellaneous items.................... | 105 69 |
| Feb. | 5.—Salaries for January.................... | 773 33 |
| " | 7.—Benoit & Wood, stationery, etc........... | 24 76 |
| | Hosford & Sons, books, etc .............. | 124 35 |
| " | 29.—Miscellaneous items.................... | 75 39 |
| Mar. | 11.—Salaries for February.................. | 791 66 |
| | S. A. Holmes, photographs of caisson...... | 87 00 |
| " | 14.—Hosford & Sons, stationery............. | 64 90 |
| " | 30.—Miscellaneous items.................... | 61 17 |
| April | 8.—Salaries for March..................... | 791 66 |
| " | 30.—Miscellaneous items.................... | 112 18 |

| | | |
|---|---|---:|
| | Total....................... ............. | $22,001 22 |

### TIMBER AND LUMBER.

| 1869. | | | |
|---|---|---:|---:|
| Oct. 29. | Kingsley & Keeney, for timber purchased from T. M. Mayhew & Co. for account of New York Bridge Co.. | ............ | $46,915 56 |
| 1869. | | | |
| Nov. 15. | M. A. Wilder, Son & Co... | $1,946 64 | |
| 1870. | | | |
| Feb. 8. | "       "       " .... | 10,052 42 | |
| Apr. 4. | "       " * " .... | 16,281 57 | |
| May 2. | "       "       " .... | 25,783 25 | |
| " 9. | "       " " .... | 5,058 84 | |
| June 6. | "       "       " .... | 21,391 56 | |
| | | $80,514 28 | |
| | Less for labor............ | 100 00 | |
| | Carried forward........ | $80,414 28 | $46,915 56 |

| | | | | |
|---|---|---|---|---|
| | Brought forward....... | | $80,414 28 | $46,915 56 |
| | Amount paid Webb & Bell for labor............... | | 219 25 | |
| | | | | 80,633 53 |
| 1870. | | | | |
| Feb. 7. | T. M. Mayhew & Co...... | | $10,535 78 | |
| Mar. 7. | " " " ..... | | 4,053 20 | |
| | | | | 14,588 98 |
| 1871. | | | | |
| Apr. 3 | Snow & Richardson....... ... | | ......... | 850 22 |
| 1870. | | | | |
| Jan. 3. | N. Y. & B'klyn S. M. & L. Co.. | | $2,873 22 | |
| Apr. 4. | " " " | | 606 24 | |
| " 4. | " " " | | 86 31 | |
| May 5. | " " " | | 991 17 | |
| June 6. | " " " | | 767 56 | |
| Sept. 6. | " " " | | 751 82 | |
| Oct. 3. | " " " | | 1,319 72 | |
| Nov. 11. | " " " | | 429 81 | |
| Dec. 7. | " " " | | 1,493 94 | |
| | " " " | | 182 46 | |
| 1871. | | | | |
| Jan. 3. | " " " | | 1,852 47 | |
| Feb. 6. | " " " | | 251 75 | |
| Mar. 6. | " " " | | 212 18 | |
| Apr. 5. | " " " | | 826 80 | |
| May. 9. | " " " | | 712 91 | |
| June 6. | " " " | | 741 39 | |
| July 10. | " " " | | 568 63 | |
| Aug. 7. | " " " | | 1,039 87 | |
| Sept. 8. | " " " | | 1,183 13 | |
| Oct. 9. | " " " | | 2,540 01 | |
| Nov. 6. | " " " | | 4,679 28 | |
| Dec. 5. | " " " | | 2,337 66 | |
| 1872. | | | | |
| Jan. 9. | " " " | | 924 15 | |
| Feb. 7. | " " " | | 2,612 53 | |
| Mar. 12. | " " " | | 2,595 55 | |
| Apr. 9. | " " " | | 2,106 25 | |
| | | | | 34,686 81 |
| 1870. | | | | |
| Feb. 8. | H. N. Conklin, Son & Beers.. | | $548 68 | |
| Mar. 8. | " " | | 936 69 | |
| Apr. 5. | " " | | 270 22 | |
| May 3. | " " | | 406 18 | |
| June 7. | " " | | 1,116 93 | |
| July 6. | " " | | 747 49 | |
| | Carried forward........ | | $4,026 19 | $177,675 10 |

|  |  | Brought forward...... | $4,026 19 | $177,675 10 |
| Aug. 10. | H. N. Conklin, Son & Beers.. | | 579 86 | |
| Sept. 7. | " " | | 442 54 | |
| Oct. 10. | " " | | 474 72 | |
| Nov. 7. | " " | | 623 45 | |
| Dec. 5. | " " | | 1,625 35 | |
| 1871. | | | | |
| Jan. 3. | " " | | 865 89 | |
| Feb. 6. | " " | | 229 32 | |
| Apr. 20. | " " | | 32 36 | |
| May 8. | " " | | 500 75 | |
| July 11. | " " | | 477 58 | |
| Sept. 8. | " " | | 1,118 91 | |
| Oct. 10. | " " | | 316 77 | |
| Nov. 7. | " " | | 1,812 02 | |
| Dec. 5. | " " | | 1,256 22 | |
| 1872. | | | | |
| Jan. 8. | " " | | 979 80 | |
| Feb. 13. | " " | | 1,075 20 | |
| Mar. 12. | " " | | 616 64 | |
| Apr. 8. | " " | | 409 75 | |
| | | | | 17,463 32 |
| 1870. | | | | |
| July 7. | Jonathan Beers........... | | $18,760 75 | |
| Aug. 11. | " ........... | | 7,096 28 | |
| Sept. 12. | " ........... | | 3,826 94 | |
| | | | | 29,683 97 |
| 1870. | | | | |
| Sept. 9. | George R. Alexander...... | | $203 36 | |
| 1871. | | | | |
| Jan. 5. | " ...... | | 195 68 | |
| July 19. | " ...... | | 11 34 | |
| Nov. 6. | " ...... | | 56 32 | |
| 1872. | | | | |
| Feb. 28. | " ...... | | 6 09 | |
| Apr. 30. | " ...... | | 28 10 | |
| | | | | 500 89 |
| 1870. | | | | |
| Feb. 8. | P. M. McGovern, storage.... | | $343 02 | |
| Sept. 9. | " " ......... | | 458 60 | |
| 1871. | | | | |
| Feb. 13. | " " ......... | | 962 57 | |
| 1872. | | | | |
| Jan. 8. | " " ......... | | 749 05 | |
| | | | | 2,513 24 |
| | | Carried forward........ | ........... | $227,836 52 |

| | | |
|---|---|---|
| Brought forward......... | ............ | $227,836 52 |
| 1870. | | |
| Mar. 8. J. F. Phelps, Jr., & Co., storage of timber........... | ............ | 212 58 |
| | | |
| 1871. | | |
| July 6. Phelps & Kimpland....... | $2,500 00 | |
| " 10. " " ........ | 2,380 50 | |
| Aug. 9. " " ........ | 203 98 | |
| Sept. 8. " " ........ | 7,188 01 | |
| Oct. 9. " " ........ | 4,629 09 | |
| Nov. 6. " " ........ | 540 00 | |
| Dec. 7. " " ........ | 54 10 | |
| | | 17,495 68 |
| 1871. | | |
| July 11. D. A. Youngs.............. | ............ | 29 75 |
| | | |
| 1872. | | |
| Mar. 11. W. H. Dunn.............. | $1,153 64 | |
| Apr. 8. " .............. | 1,713 40 | |
| | | 2,867 04 |
| 1871. | | |
| Feb. 6. A. Ammerman............ | $3,936 87 | |
| Mar. 6. " ............ | 14,691 90 | |
| Apr. 3. " ............ | 10,513 96 | |
| May 2. " ............ | 13,315 96 | |
| " 6. " ............ | 7,873 03 | |
| June 6. " ............ | 10,177 07 | |
| " " ............ | 4,000 00 | |
| July 10. " ............ | 7,731 42 | |
| Oct. 9. " ............ | 11,882 32 | |
| | | 84,122 53 |
| | | $332,564 10 |

CONTINGENT EXPENSES.

1869.

Dec. 6.—W. C. Kingsley, for expenses in inspecting stone quarries. .................... $238 00

1870.

Jan. 31.—Expenses of W. A. Roebling and A. C. Keeney, to stone quarries............ 30 00

Feb. 7.—One hundred bridge pictures............ 50 00

" 14.—Kingsley and Keeney, funeral expenses of John A. Roebling, etc.............. 681 28

April 4.—R. G. Anderson, collation at launching of Brooklyn caisson ................... 523 85

Carried forward................ $1,523 13

| | | |
|---|---|---:|
| | Brought forward.......................... | $1,523 13 |
| April | 5.—Expenses of Messrs. Roebling, Allen, Huested, and Prentice, to St. Louis and return........................................... | 431 00 |
| | Hire of six tow-boats at launching of the Brooklyn caisson ....: ............... | 216 00 |
| May | 5.—Sundry items from petty cash............. | 40 25 |
| June | 30.—    "    "    " ............... | 50 50 |
| Aug. | 16.—B. D. Silliman, legal advice, etc........... | 100 00 |
| Sept. | 7.—Fifty bridge pictures.................... | 50 00 |
| Oct. | 31.—Sundry items from petty cash............. | 5 00 |
| Nov. | 8.—Framing twenty-six bridge pictures........ | 84 50 |
| Dec. | 14.—Steamer John Fuller at fire in the caisson... | 300 00 |
| " | 27.—H. C. Murphy, Jr., searching title to property bought of Union Ferry Co........... | 620 92 |
| " | 31.—Sundries from petty cash................. | 21 75 |

1871.

| | | |
|---|---|---:|
| Mar. | 9.—J. M. Turner, medical services............. | 20 00 |
| April | 4.—Two hundred bridge pictures............. | 100 00 |
| May | 2.—Framing ten bridge pictures............. | 33 50 |
| " | 17.—R. G. Anderson, collation at launching of New York caisson .................. | 562 60 |
| June | 9.—P. C. Schultz, towing caisson from Sixth street to Atlantic basin ............... | 276 00 |
| Aug. | 30.—Sundries from petty cash................ | 30 00 |
| Sept. | 6.—W. C. Kingsley, expenses in visiting stone quarries in Maine, Massachusetts, on the Hudson river and at Canajoharie...... | 350 00 |
| " | 14.—Framing ten pictures of bridge........... | 32 50 |
| Oct. | 24.—Paid families of John French and James McGarrity, killed on the work........ | 250 00 |
| Nov. | 6.—D. Burtis, Jr., for repairing canal boat sunk at Red Hook...................... | 105 39 |
| | Funeral expenses of John French and James McGarrity............................ | 96 12 |
| " | 15.—Paid to the widow of John French........ | 350 00 |
| " | 27.—Alexander McCue, legal expenses.......... | 2,500 00 |
| " | 29.—Sundries from petty cash................. | 20 00 |
| Dec. | 2.—Paid to the widow of John McGarrity..... | 400 00 |

1872.

| | | |
|---|---|---:|
| Jan. | 10.—J. T. Conklin, medical services........... | 28 00 |
| " | 31.—Widow of Cornelius McLoughlin.......... | 250 00 |
| | Expenses to Staten Island in search of Mrs. McLoughlin...................... | 8 00 |
| | Doctor's bill............................ | 1 00 |
| Feb. | 8.—Framing twelve pictures................. | 39 00 |
| " | 29.—Funeral expenses of Henry Dougherty...... | 100 00 |
| Mar. | 11.—    "    "    " J. E. Deneys.......... | 50 80 |
| " | 13.—A. H. Smith, for medical services......... | 145 00 |
| " | 30.—Sundries from petty cash................. | 25 05 |

| | | |
|---|---|---:|
| | Carried forward............................. | $9,216 01 |

| | |
|---|---:|
| Brought forward...................................... | $9,216 01 |
| April 16.—Framing twelve photographs of the works.. | 21 60 |
| " 30.—Donation to Widow French................ | 50 00 |
| To C. H. Palmer, for injuries to hand...... | 100 00 |
| Donation to Widow Enright.............. | 750 00 |
| Sundries from petty cash................. | 22 18 |
| | |
| Total...................................... | $10,159 79 |

## TOOL ACCOUNT.

1870.

| | |
|---|---:|
| Jan. 10.—A. Inslee, one wrench.................... | $4 14 |
| Sears, Leavitt & Co...................... | 204 98 |
| Davis & Riker. ..................... | 94 43 |
| " 31.—One shackel bar........................ | 7 00 |
| Feb. 14.—Webb & Bell........................... | 6 00 |
| A. Inslee............................. | 18 00 |
| March 9.—Boston Machine Co...................... | 65 00 |
| Oriental Powder Co............. | 36 00 |
| " 10.—J. Roach & Son................... | 471 20 |
| I. Woodbury....................... | 54 00 |
| Aymar, De Grauw & Co............... | 128 65 |
| " 14.—From petty cash......................... | 1 75 |
| April 4.—Fairbanks & Co........................ | 55 10 |
| E. B. Leverich & Co................... | 411 00 |
| " 5.—Sundries from petty cash............... | 29 40 |
| J. L. Jackson & Brother............... | 117 00 |
| " 6.—W. C. Bramhill & Co ................ | 136 62 |
| " 7.—I. Woodbury..................... | 196 38 |
| " ..................... | 75 00 |
| " 8.—Lindsay, Walton & Co................. | 18 98 |
| " 9.—Aymar, De Grauw & Co............... | 813 65 |
| " 20.—P. C. Coffin........................ | 159 55 |
| Burr & Co........................ | 46 48 |
| Pratt Brothers..................... | 13 20 |
| New York Belting and Packing Co........ | 41 50 |
| " 21.—W. Marlow, Jr...................... | 17 59 |
| May 2.—S. S. Townsend..................... | 80 00 |
| C. Winant.......................... | 149 25 |
| Hubbard & Whittaker............. | 706 10 |
| " 3.—A. Inslee........................ | 14 21 |
| " 4.—John Gerrity..................... | 30 50 |
| " 5.—Aymar, De Grauw & Co............. | 90 86 |
| Davis & Riker..................... | 169 48 |
| " 5.—Sundries from petty cash............. | 13 60 |
| " 7.—R. S. Place & Co..................... | 59 92 |
| " 9.—John Bunce....................... | 37 96 |
| " 13.—Clark, Wilson & Co................. | 32 69 |
| Burr & Co........................ | 19 29 |
| " 14.—P. C. Coffin...................... | 31 94 |
| | |
| Carried forward ........................ | $4,558 40 |

|  |  | Brought forward | $4,558 40 |
|---|---|---|---|
| May | 31.—Sundries from petty cash | | 59 50 |
| June | 7.—W. C. Bramhill & Co | | 124 20 |
|  | | Lindsay, Walton & Co | 71 41 |
|  | | Aymar, De Grauw & Co | 216 84 |
|  | | P. C. Coffin | 125 63 |
|  | | Pugsley & Chapman | 25 00 |
| " | 9.—Burr & Co | | 85 80 |
| " | 13.—Geo. Griffiths | | 34 00 |
| " | 14.—Sears, Leavitt & Co | | 45 03 |
|  | | Wm. Ballard, agent | 40 05 |
| " | 22.—J. J. Reimer | | 34 75 |
|  | | John Bunce | 23 54 |
|  | | Davis & Riker | 67 51 |
| " | 30.—Sundries from petty cash | | 43 35 |
| July | 6.—Burr & Co | | 575 08 |
|  | | Lindsay, Walton & Co | 325 96 |
|  | | I. E. White | 1 50 |
| " | 7.—Forge Co | | 87 59 |
| " | 20.—J. C. Brower | | 105 24 |
| " | 27.—R. Dudgeon | | 486 00 |
| " | 30.—Mulford & Co | | 6 47 |
|  | | Sundries from petty cash | 1 58 |
| Aug. | 9.—Sears, Leavitt & Co | | 110 19 |
|  | | Lindsay, Walton & Co | 19 87 |
|  | | Aymar, De Grauw & Co | 486 35 |
|  | | C. & R. Poillon | 30 00 |
|  | | Davis & Riker | 11 00 |
|  | | Burr & Co | 157 85 |
| " | 11.—Geo. Griffiths | | 38 80 |
| Aug. | 12.—J. J. Reimer & Co | | 12 00 |
| " | 13.—John Bunce | | 12 25 |
| " | 26.—Mulford & Co | | 153 48 |
| " | 27.—J. C. Brower | | 36 50 |
| " | 31.—Sundries from petty cash | | 28 90 |
| Sept. | 6.—Burr & Co | | 217 39 |
|  | | Sears, Leavitt & Co | 7 30 |
|  | | Lindsay, Walton & Co | 48 58 |
| " | 23.—J. C. Brower | | 25 65 |
|  | | Mulford & Co | 141 27 |
| Oct. | 3.—Sears, Leavitt & Co | | 282 14 |
|  | | Walton & Co | 92 29 |
|  | | Davis & Riker | 11 75 |
|  | | Burr & Co | 81 28 |
|  | | R. Dudgeon | 216 00 |
| " | 4.—W. H. Paine | | 33 50 |
| " | 31.—Sundries from petty cash | | 4 00 |
| Nov. | 7.—R. H. Allen & Co | | 21 00 |
|  | | Pugsley & Chapman | 24 00 |
| Dec. | 5.—Sears, Leavitt & Co | | 88 66 |
|  | | Atlantic Steel Works | 32 70 |
|  | | Pugsley & Chapman | 11 66 |
|  | | | |
|  | | Carried forward | $9,680 70 |

|        |                                              |        |    |
|--------|----------------------------------------------|--------|----|
|        | Brought forward                              | $9,680 | 70 |
| Dec.   | 5.—J. C. Brower                              | 14     | 40 |
|        | Burr & Co.                                   | 106    | 81 |
| "      | 8.—Wm. Porter & Sons.                        | 56     | 29 |
|        | Jersey City Tool Company.                    | 20     | 25 |
| "      | 31.—Sundries from petty cash.                | 14     | 20 |

1871.

|        |                                                  |     |    |
|--------|--------------------------------------------------|-----|----|
| Jan.   | 3.—Pugsley & Chapman                            | 56  | 64 |
|        | Sears, Leavitt & Co.                             | 92  | 50 |
| "      | 31.—Sundries from petty cash                    | 34  | 50 |
| Feb.   | 6.—Sears, Leavitt & Co.                         | 44  | 50 |
|        | Livingston & C. Manufacturing Company..          | 29  | 74 |
| "      | 28.—Sundries from petty cash                    | 5   | 85 |
| Mar.   | 31.— "          "                               | 38  | 75 |
| April  | 3.—Walton L. and M. Works.                      | 16  | 00 |
|        | Sears, Leavitt & Co.                             | 89  | 43 |
| "      | 29.—Sundries from petty cash.                   | 37  | 05 |
| May    | 8.—A. D. Bennett.                               | 18  | 00 |
|        | Sears, Leavitt & Co.                             | 44  | 78 |
|        | The J. L. Mott Iron Works.                       | 47  | 00 |
| "      | 31.—Sundries from petty cash.                   | 18  | 50 |
| June   | 5.—A. P. and M. Stephens & Co                   | 11  | 25 |
| "      | 30.—Sundries from petty cash.                   | 5   | 96 |
| July   | 10.—De Grauw, Aymar & Co.                       | 39  | 02 |
|        | Livingston and C. Manufacturing Co..             | 11  | 74 |
|        | Clark. Wilson & Co.                              | 19  | 29 |
|        | Sears. Leavitt & Co.                             | 73  | 01 |
| "      | 31.—Sundries from petty cash.                   | 23  | 40 |
| Aug.   | 7.—De Grauw, Aymar & Co.                        | 63  | 50 |
| "      | 31.—Sundries from petty cash.                   | 28  | 25 |
| Sept.  | 6.—Sears, Leavitt & Co.                         | 62  | 15 |
|        | H. A. Rogers & Co.                               | 18  | 91 |
|        | Davis & Riker.                                   | 16  | 20 |
| "      | 30.—Sundries from petty cash.                   | 47  | 93 |
| Oct.   | 9.—H. Kane.                                      | 5   | 00 |
|        | Pugsley & Chapman.                               | 44  | 72 |
|        | De Grauw, Aymar & Co.                            | 26  | 10 |
|        | Sears, Leavitt & Co.                             | 82  | 00 |
|        | R. I. Powell & Co.                               | 30  | 00 |
| "      | 31.—Sundries from petty cash.                   | 35  | 07 |
| Nov.   | 6.—John Gray & Co.                              | 39  | 33 |
|        | Sears, Leavitt & Co.                             | 121 | 62 |
|        | Pugsley & Chapman.                               | 33  | 33 |
|        | De Grauw. Aymar & Co.                            | 11  | 20 |
|        | Davis & Riker.                                   | 5   | 95 |
| "      | 29.—Sundries from petty cash.                   | 18  | 90 |
| Dec.   | 4.—Fisher & Norris.                             | 28  | 78 |
|        | Atlantic Steel Works.                            | 31  | 40 |
| "      | 4.—Livingston & C. Manufacturing Co.            | 51  | 43 |
|        | Ames Plough Co.                                  | 24  | 00 |
|        | Sears, Leavitt & Co.                             | 50  | 77 |
|        |                                                  |     |    |
|        | Carried forward.                                 | $11,526 | 10 |

| | | | | |
|---|---|---|---|---|
| | Brought forward................... | | $11,526 | 10 |
| Dec. | 4.—Davis & Riker .............. | | 104 | 52 |
| " | 30.—Sundries from petty cash........... | | 8 | 70 |

1872.

| | | | | |
|---|---|---|---|---|
| Jan. | 6.—Collins & Co........................ | | 119 | 23 |
| | J. L. Mott Iron Works.............. | | 43 | 20 |
| | A. P. & M. Stephens & Co........... | | 27 | 00 |
| | Sears, Leavitt & Co................. | | 33 | 41 |
| | John Gray & Co..................... | | 14 | 50 |
| | G. Tagliabue....................... | | 21 | 60 |
| | Atlantic Steel Works............... | | 23 | 80 |
| | Pugsley & Chapman.................. | | 309 | 69 |
| | Clark, Wilson & Co................. | | 377 | 50 |
| " | 31.—Sundries from petty cash........... | | 5 | 33 |
| Feb. | 5.—Clark, Wilson & Co................. | | 136 | 63 |
| | Pugsley & Chapman.................. | | 42 | 74 |
| | Alfred Field & Co.................. | | 156 | 33 |
| | Collins & Co ...................... | | 3 | 80 |
| | R. I. Powell & Co.................. | | 5 | 00 |
| " | 29.—Sundries from petty cash ........... | | 14 | 72 |
| Mar. | 11.—Pugsley & Chapman................. | | 152 | 37 |
| | G. R. Alexander.................... | | 12 | 00 |
| | Howard & Morse.................... | | 12 | 60 |
| | Clark, Wilson & Co................. | | 167 | 52 |
| " | 30.—Sundries from petty cash........... | | 23 | 50 |
| April | 8.—Clark, Wilson & Co................. | | 153 | 64 |
| | J. W. Kissam...................... | | 36 | 00 |
| | H. Hoyt, Jr........................ | | 63 | 75 |
| | Pugsley & Chapman.................. | | 9 | 00 |
| | R. I. Powell....................... | | 30 | 00 |

| | | | |
|---|---|---|---|
| Total.......................... | | $13,634 | 18 |

### LABOR ACCOUNT.

1870.

| | | | | |
|---|---|---|---|---|
| Jan. | 17.—Labor pay roll to January 15............ | | $718 | 18 |
| | I. E. White, labor with pile-driver....... | | 222 | 50 |
| | Edward Stearns, labor with steamer Ox..... | | 367 | 50 |
| | William Tebo, labor with mud dredger.... | | 450 | 00 |
| " | 31.—Labor pay roll to January 29............. | | 506 | 15 |
| | I. E. White, pile-driver .................. | | 240 | 00 |
| | Edward Stearns, labor with steamer Ox..... | | 56 | 25 |
| | W. M. Tebo, labor with mud dredger..... | | 1,350 | 00 |
| Feb. | 15.—Labor pay roll to February 12.......... | | 889 | 89 |
| " | 16.—W. M. Tebo, labor with two dredges...... | | 750 | 00 |
| | I. E. White, labor with two pile-drivers.... | | 207 | 50 |
| " | 28.—Labor pay roll to February 26............ | | 728 | 65 |
| | W. M. Tebo, labor with two dredges...... | | 1,400 | 00 |
| | I. E. White, labor with two pile-drivers.... | | 235 | 00 |
| Mar. | 8.—Marston & Powers, for labor............ | | 119 | 65 |
| " | 14.—Labor pay roll to March 12.............. | | 688 | 70 |

| | | | |
|---|---|---|---|
| Carried forward........ ................... | | $8,929 | 97 |

|  |  |  |
|---|---|---|
| Brought forward | $8,929 | 97 |
| Mar. 14.—I. E. White, labor with one pile-driver | 174 | 50 |
| W. M. Tebo, labor with two dredges | 2,500 | 00 |
| " 28.— " " " | 2,400 | 00 |
| I. E. White, labor with two pile-drivers | 472 | 50 |
| Labor pay roll to March 26 | 1,599 | 09 |
| April 11.— " " April 9 | 1,090 | 33 |
| T. A. Scott, divers, etc | 1,157 | 50 |
| W. M. Tebo, labor with two dredges | 2,400 | 00 |
| I. E. White, labor with two pile-drivers | 444 | 75 |
| " 25.— " " " " | 433 | 55 |
| T. A. Scott, divers, etc | 750 | 00 |
| W. M. Tebo, two dredges | 2,400 | 00 |
| Pay roll to April 23 | 1,834 | 45 |
| May 5.—D. S. Rhule, for services in April | 117 | 00 |
| " 9.—Pay roll to May 7 | 2,115 | 67 |
| T. A. Scott, divers, etc | 612 | 50 |
| I. E. White, pile-driver | 345 | 50 |
| May 9.—W. M. Tebo, dredges | 1,050 | 00 |
| " 23.—Pay roll to May 21 | 2,593 | 14 |
| June 6.— " June 4 | 3,174 | 04 |
| " 22.— " " 18 | 3,955 | 32 |
| I. E. White, pile-driver | 151 | 35 |
| Ed. Stearns, steamer Ox | 300 | 00 |
| July 2.— " " | 225 | 00 |
| Pay roll to July 2 | 4,262 | 78 |
| " 18.— " " 16 | 7,654 | 15 |
| " 30.—Sundries from petty cash | 8 | 59 |
| Aug. 1.—Pay roll to July 30 | 8,512 | 36 |
| " 16.— " August 13 | 8,248 | 16 |
| " 29.— " " 27 | 7,769 | 27 |
| Sept. 13.— " September 10 | 8,964 | 17 |
| " 26.— " " 24 | 10,144 | 74 |
| Oct. 10.— " October 8 | 9,935 | 78 |
| " 26.— " " 22 | 11,345 | 36 |
| " 31.—Sundry items from petty cash | 23 | 10 |
| Nov. 7.—Pay roll to November 5 | 12,198 | 83 |
| " 21.— " " 19 | 12,206 | 48 |
| Dec. 5.— " December 3 | 10,909 | 67 |
| " 27.— " " 17 | 7,739 | 76 |
| " 31.— " " 30 | 6,166 | 20 |
| | | |
| 1871. | | |
| | | |
| Jan. 16.—Pay roll to January 13 | 6,750 | 87 |
| " 30.— " " 27 | 5,943 | 99 |
| " 31.—Sundry labor from petty cash | 27 | 62 |
| Feb. 6.—Marston & Powers, for labor | 4 | 00 |
| " 13.—Pay roll to February 10 | 4,454 | 85 |
| " 25.— " " 24 | 4,160 | 61 |
| " 28.—Labor from petty cash | 10 | 64 |
| Mar. 11.—Pay roll to March 10 | 4,470 | 37 |
| " 25.— " " 24 | 3,323 | 62 |
| | | |
| Carried forward | $197,462 | 13 |

```
                Brought forward......................    $197,462 13
April  3.—James Binns. labor....................        27 74
  "   10.—Pay roll to April 7...................     3.309 75
April 22.—Pay roll to April 21.................     3,087 78
May    6.—        "       May 5 .............     2,630 27
  "   11.—W. M. Tebo, dredging and pumping....        210 00
  "   22.—Pay roll to May 19..................     2,937 16
June   3.—        "       June 2 .............     2,436 41
  "   17.—        "         "  16 .............     2,567 89
July  10.—A. H. Acken, for services............        450 00
  "    6.—Pay roll to June 30.................     3.097 84
  "   15.—        "·       July 14.............     3,114 74
  "   31.—        "          "  28.............     3,343 92
                Labor from petty cash............         10 00
Aug.  14.—Pay roll to August 11................     3.349 73
  "   28.—        "            "  25.............     4.314 93
Sept.  9.—        "       September 8............     5,306 00
  "   23.—        "            "   22..........     5,604 75
  "   30.—From petty cash account.............          5 00
Oct.   9.—Pay roll to October 6................     5,142 24
                M. O'Brien, labor at caisson Sept. 11 ....    25 00
  "   11.—Labor at caisson in September, rigger, etc.        34 68
  "    9.—R. I. Powell & Co., repairing pumps.....          5 50
  "   21.—Pay roll to October 20.................     5,126 65
Nov.   4.—        "       November 3.............     4.987 46
  "   18.—        "            "    17.............     6,299 52
Dec.   2.—        "       December 1.............     6,318 66
  "   16.—        "            "   15.............     6,847 04
  "   30.—        "            "   29.............     6,353 95

      1872.

Jan.  13.—Pay roll to January 11................     9,980 99
  "   27.—        "            "   25.............    11,965 35
Feb.  10.—        "       February 8.............    10,665 11
  "   24.—        "            "   22............    11,514 30
Mar.   9.—        "       March 7...............    10,990 76
  "   23.—        "            "  21.............    10,253 14
April  6.—        "       April 4...............    10.768 94
  "   20.—        "            "  18.............    10,743 85
                                                    _____
                                                    $370,289 18
      Less received for labor......................     1,226 42
                                                    _____
      Total.....................................    $369,062 76


      1870.              MACHINERY.

Mar.   7.—Hubbard & Whittaker, two boilers......    $1,350 00
                Burleigh Rock Drill Company, two com-
                    pressors ......................     5,200 00
                Kendall & Roberts, two boilers.........     1,350 00
April  4.—Hubbard & Whittaker, two boilers.......     1,350 00
                                                    _____
                Carried forward .....................    $9,250 00
```

| | | |
|---|---|---:|
| | Brought forward .......................... | $9,250 00 |
| April | 4.—Hubbard & Whittaker, extra work and material.......................... | 782 98 |
| | Burleigh Rock Drill Company, extra fixtures, etc........................ | 103 37 |
| | Burleigh Rock Drill Company, four compressors........................ | 10,400 00 |
| | Burleigh Rock Drill Company, boxing same........................... | 76 44 |
| | National Derrick Company, four derricks. | 720 00 |
| | Davis & Riker, one gauge.............. | 30 00 |
| " | 5.—J. Patten, sundries.................... | 87 12 |
| | A. Inslee,    "    .................... | 323 95 |
| " | 6.—P. Cassidy, one boiler.................. | 205 00 |
| " | 11.—T. F. Rowland, iron and labor.......... | 329 01 |
| " | 19.—J. Cumings, three pile-driver hammers.... | 273 15 |
| | P. C. Coffin, machinery oil............. | 68 20 |
| May | 2.—W. C. Bramhill & Co., packing, gaskets, etc...................... | 74 08 |
| | Hubbard & Whittaker, castings, etc..... | 1,015 04 |
| " | 3.—Burleigh Rock Drill Company, sundries and fixtures...................... | 81 50 |
| | J. A. Roebling's Sons, wire rope, etc..... | 152 40 |
| | A. Inslee, iron-work................... | 136 74 |
| | Davis & Riker, valves and fixtures....... | 289 62 |
| " | 7.—New York Belting & Packing Company, hose. rings, etc................ | 1,436 03 |
| | John Frazier, iron-work .............. | 56 30 |
| " | 10.—John Bowie, castings, zinc, etc.......... | 233 70 |
| " | 9.—Louis Osborn, one hoisting engine....... | 1,700 00 |
| " | 13.—H. R. Worthington, pumps............. | 635 00 |
| | Chas. Gregg, one heater.............. | 71 00 |
| June | 7.—J. A. Roebling's Sons, wire rope......... | 1,786 82 |
| | "          wire ropes, etc.... | 285 20 |
| | "          turn-tables........ | 69 58 |
| | W. C. Bramhill & Co., belting and packing | 9 49 |
| | John Bowie, castings................. | 36 00 |
| " | 9.—James Cumings, wheels, drums, etc...... | 260 32 |
| | E. P. Hampson. sheave and fixtures...... | 52 78 |
| " | 14.—J. O. Morse, steam whistle............. | 10 80 |
| " | 30.—Sundries from petty cash.............. | 13 00 |
| July | 6.—J. A. Roebling's Sons, wire rope........ | 525 80 |
| | Morris & Cumings, use of dredges ...... | 6,000 00 |
| | Richardson, M. & Co., one hoisting engine | 1,500 00 |
| | Jos. Wood & Co., pump............... | 35 00 |
| | J. McFarlan, Jr., cylinder............. | 60 00 |
| " | 30.—Sundries from petty cash.............. | 156 84 |
| Aug. | 9.—Wm. Taylor & Sons, two hoisting engines | 4,900 00 |
| | Morris & Cumings, use of dredger....... | 3,000 00 |
| | John Roach & Sons, iron-work.......... | 480 92 |
| | Peteler Portable Railroad Company, cars and rail track...................... | 767 13 |
| | Carried forward .......................... | $48,480 31 |

|  | Brought forward | $48,480 31 |
| Aug. | 9.— Davis & Riker, gauges and oilers | 26 50 |
|  | J. M. Grant, gas cylinders | 105 00 |
|  | W. H. Wells,    " | 105 00 |
|  | New York Oxygen Gas Company, gas cylinders | 460 00 |
| " | 10.—Avery & Witzell, gas cylinders | 554 80 |
|  | John Powers, castings | 30 89 |
| " | 12.—John Aschrofft, gauge, etc. | 30 50 |
|  | New York Belting and Packing Company, hose, couplings, etc | 172 25 |
| Sept. | 6.—Davis & Riker, anvil, drip cups, etc | 75 81 |
|  | Burleigh Rock Drill Company, drill and fixtures | 585 87 |
|  | James Binns, cars, wheels, axles, etc | 768 76 |
|  | J. A. Roebling's Sons, wire rope, etc | 343 68 |
|  | Kingsley & Keeney, railroad track | 511 25 |
| " | 10.—S. S. Townsend, one forge | 48 09 |
|  | Avery & Witzell, gas cylinders | 928 00 |
| Oct. | 3.—J. K. Ford & Co., one engine | 600 00 |
| " | 4.—Murphy & Co., pump and fixtures | 84 88 |
|  | Novelty Iron Works, gauge, etc | 57 75 |
|  | E. B. Leverich & Co., dumping cars | 450 00 |
| " | 12.—Forge Company, forge and fixtures | 73 50 |
| " | 31.—Sundries from petty cash | 6 40 |
| Nov. | 7.—Peteler Portable Railroad Company, cars, track, etc | 952 50 |
| Dec. | 5.—C. B. Hardick, pump | 192 00 |
|  | Henry Toothe & Co., valve machine | 100 00 |
|  | L. B. Tupper, grate bars | 84 08 |
|  | Louis Osborn,    " | 7 70 |
|  | Burleigh Rock Drill Company, valves and fixtures | 104 82 |
|  | A. Inslee, one engine | 225 00 |
|  | James Cumings, buckets and repairs | 574 00 |
|  | "        buckets and fixtures | 1,777 20 |
|  | "        wheels and fixtures | 116 37 |
| **1871.** |  |  |
| Jan. | 3.—Peteler Portable Railroad Company, rail track, car, etc | 371 93 |
| Feb. | 6.—Burleigh Rock Drill Company, two compressors and fixtures | 5,013 80 |
| Mar. | 6.—Burleigh Rock Drill Company, six valves. | 120 00 |
| " | 8.—G. Symnes, hoisting machine | 50 00 |
| April | 3.—Jas. Binns, truck wheels, axles, frames, etc | 617 22 |
|  | Louis Osborn, one hoisting engine | 2,300 00 |
| May | 1.—Covington & Cincinnati Bridge Company, turn-tables and fixtures | 361 50 |
| " | 8.—C. B. Hardick, steam pump | 460 00 |
|  | Peteler Portable Railroad Company, rail track, cars, etc | 602 30 |
|  | Carried forward | $68,529 57 |

| | | |
|---|---|---|
| Brought forward | $68,529 | 57 |
| May 8.—Mason & Martin, two boilers and fixtures. | 1,200 | 00 |
| June 5.—Covington & Cincinnati Bridge Company, sundry machinery | 928 | 53 |
| A. C. Keeney, pile-driver machine and boiler | 2,100 | 00 |
| July 10.—James Cumings, pile-driver hammers, etc. | 150 | 00 |
| A. C. Keeney, pile-driver machine | 1,200 | 00 |
| Aug. 7.—C. H. Delemater, sheaves, pillow blocks, etc | 199 | 47 |
| Sept. 6.—Louis Osborn, one hoisting engine, etc... | 2,405 | 00 |
| James Cumings, drums, shafts, hammers, etc | 1,233 | 35 |
| Peteler Portable Railroad Company, rail track | 322 | 07 |
| Hubbard & Whittaker, engine boiler and fixtures | 6,545 | 00 |
| Richardson, Merriam & Co., valve | 3 | 00 |
| Oct. 9.—Louis Osborn, one hoisting engine | 2,400 | 00 |
| Hubbard & Whittaker, hoisting engines.. | 2,250 | 00 |
| Peteler Portable Railroad Company, stone trucks | 155 | 50 |
| Nov. 6.—Burleigh Rock Drill Company, one com- pressor and fixtures | 2,529 | 00 |
| Burleigh Rock Drill Company, three com- pressors and fixtures | 10,019 | 90 |
| Hubbard & Whittaker, four boilers | 2,680 | 00 |
| Dec. 4.—Peteler Portable Railroad Company, rail track, etc | 271 | 50 |
| 1872. | | |
| Jan. 6.—Peteler Portable Railroad Company, rail track, etc | 252 | 45 |
| C. B. Hardick, cylinders, etc | 118 | 50 |
| A. S. Cameron & Co., pump | 1,300 | 00 |
| Cutter, Tower & Co., valves | 136 | 80 |
| James Binns, truck wheels, axles, etc | 745 | 09 |
| Feb. 5.—C. B. Hardick, pump | 460 | 00 |
| Mar. 11.—Peteler Portable Railroad Company, turn- tables, car, etc | 180 | 03 |
| | $108,314 | 76 |
| Less discount, etc | 160 | 57 |
| Total | $108,154 | 19 |

### FREIGHT, CARTAGE AND TOWAGE.

1870.

| | | |
|---|---|---|
| Mar. 7.—Freight on compressors | $140 | 60 |
| " 14.—Sundries from petty cash | 4 | 77 |
| " 25.—Freight on compressors | 180 | 00 |
| Carried forward | $325 | 37 |

|  |  |  |  |
|---|---|---|---|
| | Brought forward ...... .................. | $325 | 37 |
| April | 6.—Carting compressors and boilers......... | 151 | 75 |
| May | 5.—Sundries from petty cash.............. | 12 | 03 |
| " | 31.— " " .............. | 28 | 62 |
| June | 13.—J. D. Martin & Co., cartage and ferriage. | 49 | 00 |
| " | 30.—Sundries from petty cash.............. | 39 | 25 |
| July | 30.— " " .............. | 11 | 75 |
| Aug. | 10.—Carting gas cylinders............... | 64 | 00 |
| " | 31.—Sundries from petty cash.............. | 12 | 10 |
| Sept. | 6.—Marston & Powers, carting and weighing | | |
| | coal............................ | 39 | 73 |
| " | 9.—Carting gas tanks.................... | 112 | 00 |
| | A. C. Nickerson, towing scows......... | 162 | 00 |
| " | 30.—Sundries from petty cash.............. | 27 | 39 |
| Oct. | 5.—T. C. Murray, carting gas tanks........ | 104 | 00 |
| " | 10.—A. C. Nickerson, towing scows......... | 162 | 00 |
| " " | 31.—Sundries from petty cash.............. | 19 | 37 |
| Nov. | 8.—T. C. Murray, carting gas tanks........ | 104 | 00 |
| " | 9.—A. C. Nickerson, towing scows......... | 194 | 50 |
| " | 30.—Sundries from petty cash.............. | 10 | 90 |
| Dec. | 5.—T. C. Murray, carting gas tanks.,....... | 104 | 00 |
| " | 6.—A. C. Nickerson, towing scows......... | 192 | 50 |
| | W. M. Tebo, towing scows and use of | | |
| | steam tug....................... | 1,168 | 20 |
| " | 31.—Sundries from petty cash.............. | 15 | 10 |
| | 1871. | | |
| Jan. | 3.—A. C. Nickerson, towing scows......... | 46 | 00 |
| " | 30.—Freight on cement.................... | 3 | 75 |
| " | 31.—Sundries from petty cash.............. | 120 | 85 |
| Feb. | 6.—A. C. Nickerson, towing scows......... | 136 | 50 |
| | Marston & Powers, unloading and carting | | |
| | sand ........................... | 369 | 60 |
| " | 7.—T. C. Murray, carting gas tanks........ | 100 | 00 |
| " | 28.—Sundries from petty cash.............. | 107 | 75 |
| Mar. | 6.—A. C. Nickerson, towing scows......... | 84 | 50 |
| " | 31.—Sundries from petty cash.............. | 7 | 55 |
| April | 3.—A. C. Nickerson, towing scows......... | 119 | 50 |
| " | 8.—Cartage on machinery.................. | 96 | 40 |
| " | 17.— " engine to Red Hook........ | 36 | 75 |
| " | 25.— " machinery................. | 150 | 00 |
| " | 29.—Sundries from petty cash.............. | 7 | 10 |
| May | 8.—A. C. Nickerson, towing scows......... | 145 | 50 |
| " | 9.—J. D. Martin & Co., cartage and ferriage | | |
| | on plank, etc.................... | 145 | 50 |
| " | 11.—W. M. Tebo, towing scows........... | 306 | 00 |
| " | 31.—Sundries from petty cash.............. | 46 | 27 |
| June | 5.—A. C. Nickerson, towing scows......... | 207 | 00 |
| " | 6.—Tow boat S. A. Stevens, caisson........ | 48 | 00 |
| " | 7.—J. E. Moore, towing caisson............ | 252 | 00 |
| " | 30.—Sundries from petty cash.............. | 21 | 00 |
| July | 10.—A. C. Nickerson, towing scows......... | 163 | 50 |
| | Carried forward ......................... | $5,830 | 58 |

```
              Brought forward .........................     $5,830 58
July  31.—Sundries from petty cash...............          5 70
Aug.   7.—A. C. Nickerson, towing scows..........        235 50
Sept.  5.—Freight on air-compressors..............       208 00
  "   30.—A. C. Nickerson, towing scows..........        121 00
              Sundries from petty cash...............      15 50
Oct.  13.—J. E. Moore, towing caisson.............       468 00
  "    9.—A. C. Nickerson, towing scows..........        360 00
  "   31.—Sundries from petty cash...............         64 80
Nov.   6.—A. C. Nickerson, towing scows..........        126 00
  "   29.—Sundries from petty cash...............        111 57
Dec.   4.—A. C. Nickerson, towing scows..........        295 00
  "   30.—Sundries from petty cash...............         11 75

      1872.

Jan.   6.—A. C. Nickerson, towing scows..........       372 00
  "   31.—Sundries from petty cash...............         24 87
Feb,   5.—A. C. Nickerson, towing scows..........       304 50
  "   29.—Sundries from petty cash...............         26 50
Mar.  11.—A. C. Nickerson, towing scows..........       635 00
  "   30.—Sundries from petty cash...............         29 79
April  8.—A. C. Nickerson, towing scows..........       389 00
                                                        _____
                                                        $9,635 06
Less charged J. Roach & Son.....................          18 00
                                                        _____
      Total.......................................      $9,617 06
```

### PRINTING AND ADVERTISING.

```
      1870.
Mar.   9.—I. Van Anden, printing reports of Chief
              Engineer, etc....................          $142 82
April  6.— Brooklyn Eagle, printing reports of Chief
              Engineer.......................            137 50
May    5.—Sundries from petty cash.............           16 30
  "   31.—Advertising notice of election..........       322 98
June   6.—     "           "          "    ..........     24 00
              "           "          "    ..........      28 00
Aug.  31.—Sundries from petty cash..............          15 63
Sept.  7.—Brooklyn Eagle, printing specifications,etc    149 50
Oct.  31.—Sundries from petty cash..............             75
Dec.  31.—     "           "          "    ..............   1 60

      1871.
June   6.—Advertising notice of election..........       200 20
  "   13.—     "           "          "    ..........     23 20
  "   30.—     "           "          "    ..........     16 53
              Sundries from petty cash..............      13 50
                                                        _____
      Total .....................................       $1,092 51
```

LAND, LAND DAMAGES, AND BUILDINGS.

1870.

| | | |
|---|---|---|
| April 11.—Union Ferry Company.................. | $68,325 | 98 |
| Aug. 10.—Charles E. Butler, on account of south half of Pier 29...................... | 5,000 | 00 |
| Oct. 10.—Balance on account of south half of Pier 29, and interest.................. | 65,847 | 67 |

1871.

| | | |
|---|---|---|
| Aug. 9.—W. H. Marston, on account of purchase of property occupied as a coal yard.... | 80,000 | 00 |
| Aug. 17.—New York & Brooklyn Ferry Company for property at Pier 29, bought of the city of New York................ | 80,000 | 00 |
| Sept. 8.—New York & Brooklyn Ferry Company for buildings and fixtures at Pier 29. | 3,500 | 00 |
| Feb. 18.—John L. Brown, on account of property bought of the city of New York at Pier 29........................ | 15,000 | 00 |

1872.

| | | |
|---|---|---|
| Feb. 20.—John L. Brown, on account of property bought of the city of New York at Pier 29........................ | 15,000 | 00 |
| Total...................................... | $332,673 | 65 |

| | |
|---|---|
| Amount due on property bought of W. H. Marston........................... | $50,000 |
| Amount due John L. Brown, on property bought of the city of New York...... | 30,000 |
| Amount due the city of New York, on property bought of them, located in Brooklyn........................... | 160,000 |
| Amount due the city of New York, on property at Pier 29................. | 42,000 |

| | |
|---|---|
| Amount due the Bridge Company, from the city of New York, for installments on capital stock.................... | $202,000 |

LIMESTONE.

| 1870. | | | | | |
|---|---|---|---|---|---|
| June | 6. | Noone & Company........ | | $2,474 | 15 |
| July | 5. | " | " | 625 | 00 |
| " | 20. | " | " | 5,756 | 16 |
| Aug. | 9. | " | " | 82 | 05 |
| " | 10. | " | " | 8,842 | 62 |
| Sept. | 5. | " | " | 11,383 | 16 |
| | | Carried forward.......... | | $29,163 | 14 |

| | | | |
|---|---|---|---|
| 1870. | Brought forward......... | $29,163 14 | |
| Oct. 18. | Noone & Company ........ | 14,966 77 | |
| Nov. 9. | " " ........ | 15,402 34 | |
| Dec. 5. | " " ........ | 307 10 | |
| " 7. | " " ........ | 23,910 65 | |
| 1871. | ........ | | |
| Jan. 3. | " " ........ | 20 03 | |
| " 19. | " " ........ | 12,155 14 | |
| Nov. 10. | " " ........ | 4,380 09 | |
| Dec. 13. | " " ........ | 6,645 92 | |
| 1872. | ........ | | |
| Jan. 10. | " " ........ | 2,730 39 | |
| Feb. 7. | " " ........ | 2,427 60 | |
| | | | $112,109 17 |
| 1871. | | | |
| Sept. 9. | Read & Morrell .......... | $2,197 98 | |
| Oct. 12. | " " .......... | 3,058 30 | |
| Nov. 8. | " " .......... | 6,578 94 | |
| Dec. 6. | " " .......... | 2,388 37 | |
| 1872. | | | |
| Jan. 12. | " " .......... | 1,161 35 | |
| | " " .......... | 2,714 98 | |
| Feb. 9. | " " .......... | 1,039 25 | |
| | | | 19,139 17 |
| 1871. | | | |
| Oct. 11. | Lake Champ. Bluestone Co. | $8,167 63 | |
| Nov. 10. | " " " | 12,892 17 | |
| Dec. 11. | " " " | 4,988 50 | |
| 1872. | | | |
| Jan. 9. | " " " | 7,976 14 | |
| Feb. 6. | " " " | 6,004 31 | |
| | | | 40,028 75 |
| | Total ................. | .......... | $171,277 09 |

INSURANCE.

1870.

Feb. 16.—Insurance on the Brooklyn caisson....... $370 00

1872.

Feb. 10.- Insurance on property bought of W. H.
Marston....................... 446 87
Insurance on property at Pier 29, N. Y... 625 00

Total..................................... $1,441 87

TAXES.

1870.

Dec. 27.—On property bought of the city of New
York, at Fulton Ferry, Brooklyn, for
1870....................................... $625 16
On property bought of Union Ferry Company, for 1870.................... 618 98

1871.

Feb. 1.—On south half of Pier 29, for 1870....... 157 50
Nov. 18.—On property bought of W. H. Marston, for
1871....................................... 1,357 53
On property bought of Union Ferry Com-
pany, for 1871.................... 861 65
On south half of Pier 29, New York, for
1871....................................... 151 94

Total....................................... $3,772 76

SCOWS.

| 1870. | | | |
|---|---|---|---|
| April 4. | N. Y. & B'klyn S. M. & L. Co. 2 scows for carrying stones. | $7,000 00 | |
| June 6. | "         "         " | 8,800 00 | |
| | | | $15,800 00 |
| 1871. | | | |
| Nov. 6. | A. Ammerman, 1 scow...... | $4,400 00 | |
| Dec. 5. | "         " ...... | 4,400 00 | |
| | | | 8,800 00 |
| 1872. | | | |
| Feb. 5. | Atlantic Dock Co., 1 scow.. | .......... | 2,500 00 |
| 1870. | *For Repairs.* | | |
| | Aymar, De Grauw & Co. | | |
| April 9. | 2 bbls. of tar........... | $6 50 | |
| May 5. | 8 "         "......... | 26 40 | |
| " 31. | Cuthbert & Cunningham. 1 bbl. of tar........... | 5 00 | |
| 1872. | | | |
| April 9. | D. Burtis, Jr., repairing 1 scow | 322 97 | |
| | "         "         " | 273 34 | |
| | "         "         " | 206 36 | |
| | | | 840 57 |
| | Total................ | .......... | $27,940 57 |

INTEREST.

1871.

Nov. 1.—W. H. Marston, interest on $80,000, paid
    him from Aug. 1 to Aug. 17........    $248 89

1872.

Feb. 1.—Bowery Savings Bank, on bond and mort-
    gage for $50,000, being balance due
    on property bought of W. H. Marston,
    say from Aug. 1, '71, to Feb. 1, '72..    1,750 00

    Total ..................................    $1,998 89


HORSES, WAGONS, AND HARNESS.

1870.

May 17.—David Daly, one wagon ...............    $275 00
"  30.—L. & M. Israels, one horse .............    340 00
June 21.—J. Knee, blankets, sheets, etc..........    28 50
"  30.—Repairs, etc........................    10 25
Aug. 11.—J. L. Moore, harness, etc .............    19 80
"  23.—Brewster & Co., one wagon............    460 00
Sept. 6.—One set of harness ..................    30 00
"  30.—Repairs and horse-shoeing............    19 25
Nov. 7.—E. Daly, repairs, etc., to wagon........    49 35
"  10.—J. L. Moore, repairs to harness, etc......    14 13

1871.

Jan. 5.—J. L. Moore, harness and repairs........    13 70
Mar. 31.—Repairs to harness, etc................    7 45
July 10.—E. Daly, repairs to wagon ............    19 75
Sept. 6.—J. R. Bodwell, one horse ...., ........    400 00
    One set of harness....................    75 00

    Total ......................................    $1,762 18


GRANITE.

1870.

July 29.—Bodwell, Webster & Co...............    $280 00
Aug. 20.   "    ...............    1,000 44
      "    ...............    150 00
"  25.   "    ...............    314 71
"  27.   "    ...............    400 00
"  30.   "    ...............    280 00
"  31.   "    ...............    334 00
      "    ...............    100 00
      "    ...............    17 50
Sept. 2.   "    ...............    416 28
      "    ...............    218 00
"  6.   "    ...............    5,538 66

    Carried forward .......................    $9,049 59

|  |  |  |  |  |
|---|---|---|---|---|
|  | Brought forward | | ............ | $9,049 59 |
| Sept. | 8.—Bodwell, Webster & Co | | ............ | 358 00 |
| " | 30. | " | ............ | 707 27 |
| Oct. | 6. | " | ............ | 441 68 |
| " | 13. | " | ............ | 3,720 66 |
| Nov. | 7. | " | ............ | 36 15 |
|  |  | " | ............ | 519 14 |
|  |  | " | ............ | 500 00 |
| " | 17. | " | ............ | 4,299 94 |
| " | 18. | " | ............ | 530 00 |
| " | 21. | " | ............ | 425 00 |
| Dec. | 5. | " | ............ | 81 30 |
| " | 7. | " | ............ | 2,554 03 |
|  |  | " | ............ | 164 50 |
| " | 14. | " | ............ | 321 85 |
| " | 16. | " | ............ | 600 00 |
| " | 27. | " | ............ | 474 84 |
| **1871.** |  |  |  |  |
| Jan. | 5. | " | ............ | 3,112 41 |
| Feb. | 23. | " | ............ | 534 85 |
| Mar. | 14. | " | ............ | 866 47 |
| " | 15. | " | ............ | 206 78 |
| " | 22. | " | ............ | 460 90 |
| " | 24. | " | ............ | 417 50 |
| " | 25. | " | ............ | 400 00 |
| " | 27. | " | ............ | 341 95 |
| " | 31. | " | ............ | 586 60 |
| April | 3. | " | ............ | 57 15 |
|  |  | " | ............ | 100 00 |
|  |  | " | ............ | 558 75 |
|  |  | " | ............ | 5,308 00 |
| " | 5. | " | ............ | 600 00 |
| " | 6. | " | ............ | 463 75 |
|  |  | " | ............ | 340 00 |
| " | 10. | " | ............ | 54 28 |
| " | 17. | " | ............ | 971 25 |
| " | 19. | " | ............ | 655 00 |
| " | 20. | " | ............ | 851 43 |
| " | 25. | " | ............ | 368 57 |
| " | 29. | " | ............ | 538 93 |
|  |  | " | ............ | 600 00 |
| May | 2. | " | ............ | 575 00 |
| " | 3. | " | ............ | 255 14 |
|  |  | " | ............ | 300 00 |
| " | 5. | " | ............ | 619 64 |
|  |  | " | ............ | 3 20 |
| " | 6. | " | ............ | 850 18 |
| " | 9. | " | ............ | 500 00 |
|  |  | " | ............ | 11,202 13 |
|  |  | " | ............ | 13,151 11 |
| " | 16. | " | ............ | 575 00 |

Carried forward ............ $71,239 92

| | | | |
|---|---|---|---|
| | Brought forward ...... ................ | $71,239 92 |
| May | 18.—Bodwell, Webster & Co............... | 495 18 |
| " | 25. | " | ................ | 550 00 |
| " | 27. | " | ................ | 639 00 |
| " | 31. | " | ................ | 480 37 |
| | | " | ................ | 364 34 |
| | | " | ................ | 304 50 |
| June | 2. | " | ................ | 781 87 |
| " | 3. | " | ................ | 461 40 |
| " | 5. | " | ................ | 600 00 |
| | | " | ................ | 356 59 |
| | | " | ................ | 2 00 |
| | | " | ................ | 16,808 40 |
| " | 6. | " | ................ | 306 85 |
| " | 8. | " | ................ | 200 00 |
| " | 9. | " | ................ | 344 41 |
| | | " | ................ | 682 00 |
| " | 12. | " | ................ | 416 85 |
| " | 13. | " | ................ | 530 57 |
| | | " | ................ | 422 35 |
| " | 14. | " | ................ | 390 42 |
| " | 15. | " | ................ | 680 00 |
| " | 16. | " | ................ | 542 00 |
| " | 17. | " | ................ | 422 42 |
| | | " | ................ | 313 72 |
| | | " | ................ | 270 28 |
| " | 20. | " | ................ | 252 00 |
| | | " | ................ | 304 00 |
| " | 22. | " | ................ | 340 00 |
| " | 23. | " | ................ | 440 00 |
| | | " | ................ | 165 86 |
| " | 24. | " | ................ | 565 00 |
| " | 27. | " | ................ | 443 60 |
| " | 28. | " | ................ | 346 00 |
| | | " | ................ | 142 29 |
| " | 30. | " | ................ | 631 12 |
| | | " | ................ | 398 57 |
| | | " | ................ | 260 00 |
| | | " | ................ | 10 00 |
| July | 1. | " | ................ | 279 42 |
| " | 3. | " | ................ | 327 42 |
| " | 6. | " | ................ | 301 70 |
| | | " | ................ | 516 80 |
| | | " | ................ | 353 42 |
| | | " | ................ | 25,000 00 |
| " | 10. | " | ................ | 8,631 15 |
| | | " | ................ | 355 25 |
| | | " | ................ | 284 38 |
| | | " | ................ | 296 38 |
| | | " | ................ | 303 28 |
| " | 12. | " | ................ | 399 00 |
| | | " | ................ | 402 00 |
| | Carried forward ...................... | $140,354 08 |

|  |  |  | Brought forward | $140,354 08 |
|---|---|---|---|---|
| July | 12.—Bodwell, Webster & Co | | | 371 09 |
|  | " | " | | 572 00 |
| " | 15. | " | | 333 62 |
| " | 17. | " | | 460 75 |
| " | 18. | " | | 454 20 |
|  | " | " | | 293 25 |
| " | 19. | " | | 355 00 |
| " | 21. | " | | 374 00 |
|  | " | " | | 306 25 |
| " | 22. | " | | 225 00 |
|  | " | " | | 318 88 |
| " | 24. | " | | 40 18 |
| " | 25. | " | | 408 88 |
| " | 26. | " | | 198 42 |
| " | 27. | " | | 263 42 |
|  | " | " | | 286 42 |
| " | 28. | " | | 416 25 |
|  | " | " | | 50 00 |
| " | 29. | " | | 332 14 |
| " | 31. | " | | 84 00 |
|  | " | " | | 206 63 |
|  | " | " | | 222 13 |
|  | " | " | | 1 40 |
| Aug. | 4. | " | | 582 50 |
| " | 7. | " | | 30,291 85 |
| " | 10. | " | | 239 57 |
| " | 14. | " | | 248 00 |
| " | 16. | " | | 320 63 |
|  | " | " | | 319 00 |
|  | " | " | | 304 62 |
|  | " | " | | 306 00 |
| " | 17. | " | | 280 25 |
| " | 18. | " | | 452 57 |
| " | 19. | " | | 362 87 |
| " | 21. | " | | 641 75 |
| " | 23. | " | | 255 00 |
| " | 24. | " | | 774 88 |
| " | 25. | " | | 445 13 |
| " | 26. | " | | 301 25 |
| " | 28. | " | | 302 50 |
|  | " | " | | 98 00 |
| " | 29. | " | | 339 38 |
|  | " | " | | 384 25 |
|  | " | " | | 429 50 |
| " | 30. | " | | 425 00 |
| " | 31. | " | | 554 75 |
| Sept. | 7. | " | | 10,000 00 |
|  | " | " | | 17,784 22 |
|  | " | " | | 200 00 |
| " | 8. | " | | 576 00 |
| " | 9. | " | | 20,000 00 |
|  |  |  | Carried forward | $234,147 46 |

|  |  |  |  |  |  |
|---|---|---|---|---|---|
| | Brought forward | | | $337,826 | 64 |
| Jan. | 8.—Bodwell, Webster & Co | | | 4,687 | 76 |
| | " | " | | 15,173 | 77 |
| " | 9. | " | | 858 | 00 |
| | | " | | 687 | 73 |
| " | 10. | " | | 125 | 00 |
| " | 20. | " | | 341 | 57 |
| Feb. | 15. | " | | 4,829 | 10 |
| March | 9. | " | | 500 | 00 |
| " | 30. | " | | 935 | 43 |
| April | 4. | " | | 482 | 32 |
| " | 27. | " | | 5,264 | 30 |

|  |  |
|---|---|
| | $371,711 62 |
| Less amount paid A. H. Acken, for services, etc | 366 00 |
| | $371,345 62 |

1872.

Jan.    9.—C. P. Dixon ............................ 611 82

Total ...................................... $371,957 44

1869.                    OFFICE FURNITURE.

| | | |
|---|---|---|
| Dec. | 6.—Stewart & Co., carpets | $217 32 |
| | J. W. Vandewater, desks, etc | 315 00 |
| | T. Brooks & Co., window shades | 34 50 |

1870.

| | | |
|---|---|---|
| Jan. | 11.—E. M. Hendrickson, iron safe | 750 00 |
| Feb. | 8.—Kingsley & Keeney, desks, tables, chairs, carpets, etc | 1,459 83 |
| " | 28.—Three tables and twelve chairs | 100 00 |
| Mar. | 14.—Miscellaneous items | 22 31 |
| April | 5. " | 20 80 |
| " | 7.—J. W. Vandewater, desks, chairs, tables, couch, alterations, etc | 923 00 |
| " | 19.—Stewart, Sutphen & Co., carpets, shades, mats, etc | 316 31 |
| May | 5.—Miscellaneous items | 27 65 |
| " | 31. " | 29 50 |
| June | 11.—James Scott, chest of drawers | 95 64 |
| " | 29.—George Wilson, one desk and five chairs | 56 00 |
| " | 30.—Miscellaneous items | 49 75 |
| Aug. | 10.—Stewart, Sutphen & Co., matting, shades, etc | 82 28 |
| " | 12.—J. J. Reimer & Co., two mats | 3 00 |
| " | 13.—John Bunce, sundries | 15 00 |
| Oct. | 4.—Picture frames and cord | 23 19 |
| Dec. | 5.—Richardson, Boynton & Co., stoves and fixtures | 102 62 |

Carried forward ............................ $4,643 70

|  | Brought forward | $4,643 70 |
| Dec. | 9.—D. Armstrong, stoves and fixtures | 40 20 |
|  | Brien, Adams & Brien, gas fixtures | 211 70 |

1871.

| Jan. | 31.—Oil cloth | 8 25 |
| April | 29.—Miscellaneous items | 9 25 |
| July | 10.—R. I. Powell, water cooler | 6 75 |
| Oct. | 11.—J. W. Vandewater, six chairs | 18 00 |
| " | 31.—Miscellaneous items | 49 73 |
| Nov. | 6.—J. W. Vandewater, desk, chair | 37 75 |
|  | C. C. Martin, two stoves and fixtures | 45 00 |
| Dec. | 4.—J. W. Vandewater, desks, chairs and shades | 69 00 |
|  | Richardson, Boynton & Co., stoves and fixtures | 34 50 |
| " | 30.—Miscellaneous items | 3 25 |

1872.

| Jan. | 6.—Foster Brothers, matting and mat | 64 80 |
| " | 31.—Miscellaneous items | 5 05 |
| Feb. | 5.—J. L. Mott Iron Works, two stoves | 24 30 |
|  | J. W. Vandewater, twelve chairs and two couches | 66 00 |

| Total | $5,337 23 |

BONDS OF THE CITY OF NEW YORK.

1872.

Feb. 7.—New York Bridge bonds at par ......... $248,000 00

Bodwell, Webster & Co., freights paid on granite delivered in April, 1872..... $2,232 71

CONSTRUCTION ACCOUNT.

*Webb & Bell.*

| Labor building Brooklyn caisson, as per contract | $70,000 00 |
| Iron-work for Brooklyn caisson | 26,265 55 |
| Labor putting on ten additional courses of timber | 13,750 00 |
| Iron-work for additional courses | 13,275 87 |
| Extra work and material ordered by Chief Engineer | 4,971 23 |

| Total | $128,262 65 |

47

| 1869. | | | |
|---|---|---|---|
| Dec. 9. | Cash paid Webb & Bell..... | $6,551 06 | |
| 1870. | | | |
| Jan. 10. | " " ..... | 20,591 66 | |
| Feb. 10. | " " ..... | 26,140 28 | |
| " 14. | " " ..... | 1,024 79 | |
| Mar. 9. | " " ..... | 18,834 04 | |
| April 5. | " " ..... | 27,126 68 | |
| May 17. | " " ..... | 6,409 27 | |
| June 6. | " " ..... | 16,029 90 | |
| July 6. | " " ..... | 5,554 97 | |
| | | | $128,262 65 |

*Webb & Bell.*

| | | |
|---|---|---|
| Labor building New York caisson, as per contract | $43,000 00 | |
| Iron-work for New York caisson.............. | 29,736 57 | |
| Scarping timber of caisson. | 2,000 00 | |
| Caulking caisson......... | 3,200 00 | |
| Tinning caisson.......... | 3,000 00 | |
| Extra labor and material ordered by Chief Engineer............... | 3,821 20 | |
| Total .............. | $84,757 77 | |

| 1870. | | | |
|---|---|---|---|
| Nov. 10. | Cash paid Webb & Bell..... | $5,749 06 | |
| Dec. 6. | " " ..... | 9,340 15 | |
| 1871. | | | |
| Jan. 7. | " " ..... | 1,211 58 | |
| Feb. 10. | " " ..... | 2,024 90 | |
| Mar. 8. | " " ..... | 4,322 02 | |
| April 6. | " " ..... | 16,911 72 | |
| May 2. | " " ..... | 6,700 00 | |
| " 15. | " " ..... | 30,000 00 | |
| June 5. | " " ..... | 8,498 34 | |
| | | | 84,757 77 |
| | | | $213,020 42 |

*John Roach & Son.*

| 1870. | | | |
|---|---|---|---|
| May | 2. | Air, water, and supply shafts | $1,402 38 |
| June | 7. | Air locks, water and supply shafts, iron-work, etc.. | 4,675 52 |
| July | 6. | Water shaft, etc............ | 1,586 06 |
| Sept. | 23. | Iron-work................. | 43 60 |

$7,707 56

| | |
|---|---|
| Iron-work for the New York caisson, as per contract | $35,005 05 |
| Water shafts, air shafts, supply shafts, air locks, and extra labor and material............. | 11,495 76 |
| Total............... | $46,500 81 |

| 1870. | | | |
|---|---|---|---|
| Nov. | 10. | Cash paid John Roach & Son | $3,580 42 |
| Dec. | 8. | "           " | 5,220 69 |
| 1871. | | | |
| Jan. | 5. | "           " | 8,239 24 |
| Feb. | 8. | "           " | 7,441 11 |
| Mar. | 7. | "           " | 2,020 11 |
| April | 4. | "           " | 555 50 |
| May | 1. | "           " | 773 70 |
| | | "           " | 66 88 |
| " | 9. | "           " | 8,931 86 |
| June | 8. | "           " | 87 77 |
| July | 11. | "           " | 895 35 |
| Aug. | 7. | "           " | 18 00 |
| " | 8. | "           " | 1,018 00 |
| Nov. | 10. | "           " | 433 44 |
| Dec. | 5. | "           " | 936 54 |
| 1872. | | | |
| Jan. | 8. | "           " | 3,940 35 |
| Feb. | 7. | "           " | 2,341 85 |

40,500 81

| Total................ | | | $54,208 37 |
|---|---|---|---|

*Hubbard & Whittaker.*

| | |
|---|---|
| Iron-work for Brooklyn caisson, as per contract | $9,087 92 |
| Extra labor and material... | 325 77 |
| Total................ | $9,413 69 |

| 1869. | | | | |
|---|---|---|---|---|
| Dec. 9. | Cash paid Hubbard & Whittaker | $673 76 | | |
| 1870. | | | | |
| Feb. 8. | " " .... | 312 25 | | |
| | " " .... | 4,333 58 | | |
| Mar. 7. | " " .... | 4,094 10 | | |
| | | | $9,413 69 | |
| May 2. | " " .... | $657 88 | | |
| June 13. | " " .... | 402 56 | | |
| July 5. | Cash paid for iron-work, ordered by Engineer | 312 35 | | |
| Aug. 10. | " " .... | 277 30 | | |
| Sept. 7. | " " .... | 93 56 | | |
| Oct. 5. | " " .... | 53 92 | | |
| Dec. 5. | " " .... | 367 46 | | |
| 1871. | | | | |
| Jan. 4. | " " ,.... | 172 22 | | |
| Feb. 6. | " " .... | 340 63 | | |
| Mar. 9. | " " .... | 136 76 | | |
| May 8. | " " .... | 360 41 | | |
| June 5. | " " .... | 94 94 | | |
| July 10. | " " .... | 295 99 | | |
| Aug. 8. | " " .... | 911 08 | | |
| Sept. 8. | " " .... | 945 29 | | |
| Oct. 9. | " " .... | 567 10 | | |
| Nov. 6. | " " .... | 1,708 77 | | |
| Dec. 5. | " " .... | 572 84 | | |
| 1872. | | | | |
| Jan. 6. | " " ... | 339 92 | | |
| Feb. 5. | " " .... | 570 34 | | |
| Mar. 11. | " " .... | 553 07 | | |
| April 10. | " " .... | 340 77 | | |
| | | | 10,075 16 | |
| | | | $19,488 85 | |

*Divine Burtis, Jr., as per contract.*

| Labor putting on seventeen courses of timber on the N. Y. caisson, seven at $1,400, and ten at $1,125 | $21,050 00 |
|---|---|
| Building coffer-dam | 2,000 00 |
| Iron-work on caisson | 31,754 44 |
| Extra work and material | 1,069 48 |
| Total | $55,873 92 |

Building and caulking cof-
    fer-dam .............. $7,000 00
Iron-work on coffer-dam... 8,051 31

    Total................ $15,051 31

For extra labor and material  $4,823 56

Unpaid May 1, $4,357 31

| 1871. | | | |
|---|---|---|---|
| July 11. | Cash paid Divine Burtis, Jr. | $4,808 20 | |
| Aug. 8. | " " | 10,546 08 | |
| Sept. 8. | " " | 4,483 59 | |
| Oct. 9. | " " | 9,384 95 | |
| Nov. 6. | " " | 30,600 28 | |
| Dec. 6. | " " | 863 60 | |
| 1872. | | | |
| Jan. 8. | " " | 2,153 60 | |
| Feb. 6. | " " | 2,268 40 | |
| Mar. 12. | " " | 874 38 | |
| April 9. | " " | 2,697 34 | |
| " 9. | " " | 2,711 06 | |
| | | | $71,391 48 |

1870.                 *Marston & Powers.*

| | | |
|---|---|---|
| May 13.—Coal............................... | | $19 50 |
| June 6. " ................................ | | 293 00 |
| July 6. " ................................ | | 473 75 |
| Aug. 10. " ................................ | | 424 25 |
| Sept. 7. " ................................ | | 835 50 |
| Oct. 5. " ................................ | | 430 55 |
| Nov. 8. " ................................ | | 1,765 00 |
| Unloading gravel and sand............ | | 162 15 |
| Dec. 6.—Coal............................... | | 2,042 58 |
| 1871. | | |
| Jan. 4.—Coal............................... | | 1,497 05 |
| Feb. 7. " and unloading gravel and sand..... | | 1,053 70 |
| Mar. 8. " ................................ | | 910 50 |
| April 10. " ................................ | | 103 00 |
| May 10. " and unloading sand............... | | 302 30 |
| June 8. " ................................ | | 237 00 |
| Cartage, and unloading sand and gravel. | | 68 70 |
| July 11.—Coal............................... | | 268 75 |
| Aug. 9. " .................... .......... | | 298 25 |
| Sept. 9. " ................................ | | 327 00 |
| Unloading gravel.................. | | 99 30 |
| Carried forward....................... | | $11,611 83 |

|  |  |  |  |
|---|---|---|---|
| Brought forward | | | $11,611 83 |
| Oct. 10.—Coal | | | 458 75 |
| Nov. 8. | " | | 336 88 |
| Dec. 7. | " and unloading sand and gravel | | 101 27 |
| 1872. | | | |
| Mar. 11.—Unloading sand | | | 92 40 |
| Coal | | | 2,345 00 |
| April 9. | " | | 1,655 40 |
| Total | | | $16,601 53 |

1870. *Mason & Watts.*

|  |  |  |  |
|---|---|---|---|
| June | 6.—Sand and gravel | | $2,441 60 |
| July | 6. | " | 1,737 17 |
| Aug. | 10. | " | 405 93 |
| Sept. | 9. | " | 786 08 |
| Oct. | 6. | " | 2,131 02 |
| Nov. | 11. | " | 1,905 93 |
| Dec. | 6. | " | 990 31 |
| 1871. | | | |
| Jan. | 4. | " | 1,729 66 |
| Feb. | 8. | " | 2,323 32 |
| Mar. | 8. | " | 93 43 |
| April | 6. | " | 135 38 |
| May | 9. | " | 738 60 |
| June | 10. | " | 234 15 |
| July | 13. | " | 352 15 |
| Aug. | 12. | " | 203 40 |
| Sept. | 8. | " | 349 50 |
| Oct. | 12. | " | 707 62 |
| Nov. | 14. | " | 2,026 40 |
| Dec. | 7. | " | 2,050 35 |
| 1872. | | | |
| Jan. | 9. | " | 1,769 90 |
| Feb. | 8. | " | 1,018 10 |
| April | 9. | " | 712 30 |
| Total | | | $24,841 70 |

1870. *R. S. Place & Co.*

|  |  |  |  |
|---|---|---|---|
| May | 7.—Iron-work | | $328 66 |
| June | 9. | " | 391 14 |
| July | 12. | " | 484 46 |
| Aug. | 16. | " | 81 27 |
| Sept. | 13. | " | 110 74 |
| Oct. | 8. | " | 204 69 |
| Nov. | 10. | " | 211 99 |
| Dec. | 9. | " | 129 91 |
| Carried forward | | | $1,942 86 |

|  |  | Brought forward............................ | $1,942 86 |
| --- | --- | --- | --- |
| 1871. |  |  |  |
| Jan. | 7.—Iron-work..................... | | 143 58 |
| Feb. | 8. | " ............................ | 346 16 |
| Mar. | 7. | " ............................ | 115 09 |
| April | 7. | " ............................ | 23 86 |
| May | 9. | " ............................ | 44 55 |
| June | 8. | " ............................ | 116 93 |
| July | 13. | " ............................ | 286 54 |
| Aug. | 9. | " ............................ | 410 17 |
| Sept. | 8. | " ............................ | 606 92 |
| Oct. | 10. | " ............................ | 1,331 45 |
| Nov. | 9. | " ............................ | 1,787 72 |
| Dec. | 9. | " ............................ | 356 85 |
| 1872. |  |  |  |
| Jan. | 10. | " ............................ | 405 30 |
| Feb. | 13. | " ............................ | 541 45 |
| Mar. | 12. | " ............................ | 392 39 |
| April 12. | | " ............................ | 275 20 |
|  | Total................................... | | $9,127 02 |

| 1870. | | *Egleston Brothers & Co.* | |
| --- | --- | --- | --- |
| June | 8.—Iron and steel..................... | | $87 60 |
| Aug. | 11. | " ............................ | 269 56 |
| Sept. | 9. | " ............................ | 177 12 |
| Oct. | 10. | " ............................ | 219 32 |
| Nov. | 7. | " ............................ | 185 47 |
| Dec. | 9. | " ............................ | 388 22 |
| 1871. |  |  |  |
| Jan. | 19. | " ............................ | 146 68 |
| Feb. | 7. | " ............................ | 215 42 |
| Mar. | 14. | " ............................ | 483 73 |
| April 11. | | " ............................ | 353 14 |
| May | 16. | " ............................ | 98 92 |
| July | 19.. | " ............................ | 496 98 |
| Aug. | 10. | " ............................ | 420 69 |
| Sept. | 8. | " ............................ | 103 05 |
| Oct. | 10. | " ............................ | 350 73 |
| Nov. | 8. | " ............................ | 237 10 |
| Dec. | 12. | " ............................ | 1,613 37 |
| 1872. |  |  |  |
| Jan. | 12. | " ............................ | 100 24 |
| Feb. | 13. | " ............................ | 580 91 |
| Mar. | 15. | " ............................ | 616 03 |
| April 11. | | " ............................ | 322 02 |
| 1870. |  |  |  |
| July | 18. | " ............................ | 357 00 |
|  | Total................................... | | $7,823 30 |

1870.                     *James O. Morse.*

| | | |
|---|---|---|
| May 13.—Iron pipes and fittings | | $45 16 |
| June 14. | " | 50 70 |
| Aug. 23. | " | 27 25 |

1871.

| Jan. 19. | " | 52 25 |
|---|---|---|
| Feb. 17. | " | 37 98 |
| April 6. | " | 1,286 59 |
| May 12. | " | 116 91 |
| June 19. | " | 440 51 |
| Aug. 10. | " | 39 00 |
| Oct. 11. | " | 991 01 |
| Nov. 9. | " | 1,099 83 |
| Dec. 11. | " | 1,199 91 |

1872.

| Jan. 9. | " | 1,150 25 |
|---|---|---|
| Feb. 6. | " | 1,330 72 |
| Mar. 12. | " | 1,260 67 |
| April 11. | " | 477 05 |

Total.................................    $9,605 79

1870.                     *Sanderson Brothers & Co.*

| Sept. 20.—Steel | | $90 01 |
|---|---|---|
| Oct. 26. | " | 83 22 |
| Nov. 18. | " | 25 39 |
| Dec. 8. | " | 17 15 |

1871.

| Mar. 8. | " | 90 15 |
|---|---|---|
| April 6. | " | 50 13 |
| May 12. | " | 65 03 |
| June 19. | " | 14 83 |
| Dec. 12. | " | 134 91 |

1872.

| Jan. 18. | " | 14 00 |
|---|---|---|
| Mar. 14. | " | 47 16 |
| April 9. | " | 118 36 |

Total.................................    $750 34

1870.                     *Aymar, De Grauw & Co.*

| June 8.—Coal, tar, packing waste, oakum, etc | | $42 25 |
|---|---|---|
| Sept. 10.—Rope, chain, waste, etc | | 309 44 |
| Oct. 5. " oakum, " | | 382 95 |

Carried forward .........................    $734 64

|                                                        |           |
|--------------------------------------------------------|-----------|
| Brought forward                                        | $734 64   |
| Nov. 16.—Waste, marline, etc.                          | 56 04     |
| Dec. 7. " oakum, etc.                                  | 36 83     |

1871.

|                                                        |           |
|--------------------------------------------------------|-----------|
| Jan. 6.—Waste and tallow                               | 19 65     |
| Feb. 7.—Rope, waste, packing, etc.                     | 160 52    |

1870.

|                                                        |           |
|--------------------------------------------------------|-----------|
| July 12.—Rope, chains, etc.                            | 406 57    |

1871.                   *De Grauw, Aymar & Co.*

|                                                        |           |
|--------------------------------------------------------|-----------|
| Mar. 11.—Rope and oakum                                | 657 13    |
| April 5.   "   waste, etc.                             | 100 89    |
| May 22.    "   etc.                                    | 148 92    |
| June 10.   "   etc.                                    | 636 44    |
| July 11.   "   spikes, and old sails, etc.             | 667 21    |
| Aug. 9.    "   spikes and tallow                       | 1,004 86  |
| Sept. 9.   "   waste, etc.                             | 963 74    |
| Oct. 11.   "   spikes, waste, etc.                     | 847 46    |
| Nov. 8.    "       "                                   | 2,272 73  |
| Dec. 5.    "   marline, etc.                           | 1,008 74  |

1872.

|                                                        |           |
|--------------------------------------------------------|-----------|
| Jan. 9.    "   packing, etc.                           | 829 08    |
| Feb. 8.    "       "                                   | 566 61    |
| Mar. 12.   "       "                                   | 606 60    |
| April 9.   "       "                                   | 652 42    |
|                                                        |           |
| Total                                                  | $12,377 08 |

1870.                   *John A. Roebling's Sons.*

|                                                        |           |
|--------------------------------------------------------|-----------|
| Oct. 4.—Wire rope, sockets, etc.                       | $256 75   |
| " 31.—Freight                                          | 2 29      |
| Nov. 8.—Wire rope, sockets, etc.                       | 552 46    |
| " 30.—Freight                                          | 4 07      |
| Dec. 7.—Wire rope, etc.                                | 443 49    |
| " 31.—Freight                                          | 2 08      |

1871.

|                                                        |           |
|--------------------------------------------------------|-----------|
| Jan. 6.—Wire rope, etc.                                | 222 46    |
| " 31.—Freight                                          | 3 73      |
| Feb. 28.    "                                          | 11 78     |
| Mar. 9.—Wire rope, etc.                                | 793 57    |
| May 12.     "                                          | 133 06    |
| June 30.—Freight                                       | 2 29      |
| July 10.—Wire rope                                     | 95 27     |
| " 31.—Freight                                          | 2 38      |
| Aug. 7.—Wire rope                                      | 124 79    |
| Sept. 11.    "                                         | 70 79     |
| " 30.—Freight                                          | 69        |
|                                                        |           |
| Carried forward                                        | $2,721 95 |

| | | |
|---|---|---:|
| Brought forward ...... ................. | | $2,721 95 |
| Oct. 10.—Wire rope........................... | | 18 50 |
| " 30.—Freight............................ | | 14 26 |
| Nov. 6.—Wire rope........................... | | 919 51 |
| Dec. 8. " ......................... | | 467 09 |
| " 30.—Freight............................ | | 16 72 |

1872.

| | | |
|---|---|---:|
| Jan. 9.—Wire rope........................... | | 626 70 |
| " 31.—Freight............................ | | 1 63 |
| Mar. 14.—Wire rope........................... | | 965 10 |
| April 9. " ......................... | | 74 52 |

| | | |
|---|---|---:|
| Total ................................. | | $5,825 98 |

1870.                           *Burr & Co.*

| | | |
|---|---|---:|
| Oct. 13.—Sheaves, pins, etc..................... | | $36 77 |
| Nov. 11.—Blocks, etc......................... | | 284 05 |

1871.

| | | |
|---|---|---:|
| Jan. 14. " ......................... | | 39 60 |
| Mar. 11. " ......................... | | 444 70 |
| April 13. " ......................... | | 33 66 |
| May 9. " ......................... | | 76 04 |
| June 14. " ......................... | | 56 16 |
| July 19. " ......................... | | 72 75 |
| Sept. 12. " ......................... | | 186 24 |
| Oct. 11. " ......................... | | 160 62 |
| Nov. 11. " ......................... | | 152 59 |
| Dec. 11. " ......................... | | 137 10 |

1872.

| | | |
|---|---|---:|
| Jan. 12. " ......................... | | 205 70 |
| Feb. 13. " ......................... | | 74 67 |
| Mar. 25. " ......................... | | 25 95 |
| April 18. " ......................... | | 26 90 |

| | | |
|---|---|---:|
| Total....................... | | $2,013 50 |

1870.            *F. O. Norton—as per contract.*

| | | |
|---|---|---:|
| Aug. 11.—Cement............................. | | $1,124 80 |
| Sept. 13. " ......................... | | 1,341 25 |
| Oct. 11. " ......................... | | 518 00 |
| Nov. 15. " ......................... | | 1,739 00 |
| Dec. 6. " ......................... | | 10,167 60 |

1871.

| | | |
|---|---|---:|
| May 17. " ......................... | | 1,006 25 |
| June 5. " ......................... | | 882 00 |
| July 19. " ......................... | | 1,380 75 |
| Aug. 10. " ......................... | | 673 20 |

| | | |
|---|---|---:|
| Carried forward ...................... | | $18,832 85 |

```
        Brought forward ........................    $18,832 85
Sept. 11.—Cement.....  ........................      1,475 60
Oct.   9.    "     ............................      1,227 40
Dec. 15.    "      ............................        528 00
     1872.
Jan.  11.    "     ............................      2,161 50
                                                    ─────────
        Total........................            $24,225 35
```

1870.         *Morton, Canda & Co.—as per contract.*

```
May   3.—Cement, lime and brick...............        $591 25
June  7.—Cement ..............................      1,543 90
July  9.    "      ............................      1,920 60
     1871.
Jan.  4.—Cement, lime and brick...............      1,692 66
May   9.—Cement and lime......................      1,604 75
Aug. 17.—Cement ............. .............         97 50
Oct. 10.—Cement and brick.....................      1,679 70
Nov.  8.    "        "      ....................      3,372 95
Dec.  5.—Cement ..............................      5,007 75
     1872.
Jan. 10.—Cement and lime......................        827 25
Feb.  5.—Cement ..............................      1,845 00
```

1872.         *John Morton & Son—as per contract.*

```
Mar. 11.—Cement ..............................      4,273 05
April 8.    "      ............................      1,176 00
                                                    ─────────
        Total........................            $25,632 36
```

1870.         *A. B. Stearns & Co.—as per contract.*

```
Oct.  3.—Coal.................................     $1,124 15
Nov.  7.   "      .............................        125 20
     1871.
Dec.  4.   "      .............................        531 25
     1872.
Jan.  6.   "      .............................      2,783 16
Feb.  5.   "      .............................      1,395 10
                                                    ─────────
        Total........................             $5,958 86
```

1870.              *J. B. Carr & Co.*

```
Oct. 10.—Chains...............................         $43 18
Nov.  8.   "      .............................         33 78
Dec.  7.   "      .............................         51 74
     1871.
Feb.  7.   "      .............................         25 95
                                                    ─────────
        Carried forward ........................      $154 65
```

|  |  |  |
|---|---|---|
| Brought forward | $154 | 65 |
| April 7.—Chains | 15 | 26 |
| July 10. " | 34 | 96 |
| Aug. 7. " | 32 | 99 |

1872.

| Feb. 22. " | 76 | 02 |
|---|---|---|

| Total | $313 | 88 |
|---|---|---|

1870.                         *Abm. Inslee.*

|  |  |  |
|---|---|---|
| Jan. 10.—Iron-work | $36 | 00 |
| Feb. 15. " | 110 | 41 |
| Mar. 8. " | 227 | 26 |
| May 3. " | 193 | 66 |
| June 6. " | 68 | 75 |
| July 6. " | 61 | 33 |
| Aug. 10. " | 55 | 33 |
| Sept. 7. " | 82 | 21 |
| Oct. 4. " | 164 | 03 |
| Nov. 8. " | 161 | 09 |
| Dec. 6. " | 237 | 11 |

1871.

|  |  |  |
|---|---|---|
| Jan. 4. " | 58 | 47 |
| Feb. 7. " | 62 | 23 |
| Mar. 6. " | 138 | 52 |
| April 19. " | 25 | 71 |
| May 9. " | 47 | 66 |
| June 6.—Labor, etc | 47 | 94 |

1872.

|  |  |  |
|---|---|---|
| Jan. 31.—Iron-work | 37 | 15 |
| Feb. 7.—Labor | 18 | 00 |
| Mar. 12. " | 10 | 50 |

| Total | $1,843 | 36 |
|---|---|---|

1870.                         *A. Gross & Co.*

|  |  |  |
|---|---|---|
| June 20.—Candles | $565 | 60 |
| Sept. 7. " | 243 | 94 |
| Oct. 11. " | 554 | 40 |
| Nov. 10. " | 554 | 40 |
| Dec. 12. " | 853 | 78 |

1871.

|  |  |  |
|---|---|---|
| Jan. 7. " | 277 | 20 |
| Feb. 7. " | 280 | 00 |
| Mar. 8. " | 218 | 96 |
| June 19. " | 13 | 86 |

| Carried forward | $3,562 | 14 |
|---|---|---|

Brought forward ....................... $3,562 14
1872.

Jan. 20.—Candles............................. 299 38
Feb. 15.   "   ............................. 266 12
Mar. 25.   "   ............................. 271 66

Total....................................... $4,399 30

1870.                James W. Valentine.

July  8.—Cement and coal..................... $172 50

1870.                Sears, Leavitt & Co.

June 15.—Chains, spikes, nails, etc.............. $70 02
July 21.—Nails, spikes, etc.................... 31 46
Aug. 16.—Nails and spikes..................... 38 25
Sept. 7.—Nails, spikes, etc.................... 31 50
Oct. 10.   "    "   ....................... 93 75
Nov. 12.—Rope, shovels, nails, spikes, etc......... 732 02
Dec. 10.—Rope, nails and spikes................. 702 74

1871.

Jan. 13.   "        "   ................. 126 30
Feb. 15.   "        "   ................. 217 48
Mar. 8.—Axes............................. 17 00
April 10.—Nails........................... 26 25
June 19.—Nails and spikes..................... 17 75
July 19.—Nails........................... 23 00
Sept. 12.—Nails and spikes.................... 41 75

Total ............................... $2,169 27

1870.                Richardson, Boynton & Co.

July 29.—Steel ............................. $41 00
Aug. 26.   "   ............................. 26 56
Sept. 20.   "   ............................. 18 80
Oct. 26.   "   ............................. 29 28
Nov. 18.—Stove and fixtures................... 14 90

1871.
April 3.   "        "   ................. 10 04

1872.
Mar. 14.—Stove, boiler, etc................... 32 00

Total................................. $172 58

1870.        New York Belting and Packing Co.

July  9.—Hose, etc.......................... $94 50
Sept. 20.—Hose, couplings, etc................. 349 40
Nov. 11.—Hose, etc.......................... 86 83

Carried forward ...................... $530 73

|  |  |  |  |
|---|---|---|---|
| Brought forward | | | $530 73 |

1871.

| Jan. | 19.—Hose, etc | | 221 40 |
|---|---|---|---|
| April | 6. | " | 222 75 |
| May | 31. | " | 5 24 |
| July | 14. | " | 126 00 |
| Aug. | 10. | " | 96 94 |
| Sept. | 12. | " | 112 35 |

1872.

| Jan. | 20. | " | 105 85 |
|---|---|---|---|
| Feb. | 15. | " | 79 65 |
| Mar. | 11. | " | 96 75 |
| April | 30. | " | 1 69 |

| Total | | | $1,599 35 |
|---|---|---|---|

1870. *Brooklyn Gas-Light Co.*

| Aug. | 11.—Gas | | $100 80 |
|---|---|---|---|
| Oct. | 4. | " | 80 27 |
| Nov. | 9. | " | 88 40 |
| Dec. | 7. | " | 206 38 |

1871.

| Jan. | 5. | " | 24 37 |
|---|---|---|---|
| Feb. | 9. | " | 170 63 |
| Mar. | 7. | " | 167 05 |
| April | 4. | " | 95 22 |
| May | 2. | " | 30 23 |

| Total | | | $963 35 |
|---|---|---|---|

1870. *Holden, Hopkins & Stokes.*

| May | 3.—Iron | | $224 79 |
|---|---|---|---|
| June | 9. | " | 132 10 |

| Total | | | $356 89 |
|---|---|---|---|

1870. *Coplay Cement Co.*

| June | 9.—Cement | | $1,837 50 |
|---|---|---|---|
| Aug. | 11. | " | 105 00 |

1871.

| Feb. | 7. | " | 700 00 |
|---|---|---|---|

| Total | | | $2,642 50 |
|---|---|---|---|

1871. *Combination Rubber Co.*

| Aug. 10.—Hose and couplings | | | $48 62 |
|---|---|---|---|

| Carried forward | | | $48 62 |
|---|---|---|---|

|  | Brought forward | $48 62 |
|---|---|---|
| Sept. 12. | Packing | 22 59 |
| Oct. 12. | Hose and couplings | 48 62 |
| Nov. 21. | Hose and hose pipes | 432 00 |

1872.

| Jan. 12. | Hose, belting, packing, etc | 395 87 |
|---|---|---|
| Feb. 15. | Hose | 235 88 |
| Mar. 13. | Hose, packing and couplings | 215 35 |

| Total | $1,398 93 |
|---|---|

1870. *Pool & Bergen.*

| May 3. | Oil, paints, lamps, glasses, etc | $23 43 |
|---|---|---|
| June 6. | "     "     "     " | 34 40 |

1870. *George Pool & Sons.*

| Aug. 11. | Paints, oils, lanterns, varnish, etc | 78 41 |
|---|---|---|
| Sept. 13. | "     "     " | 36 13 |
| Oct. 5. | "     "     " | 87 00 |
| Nov. 9. | "     "     " | 118 19 |
| Dec. 12. | "     "     " | 83 19 |

1871.

| Jan. 5. | "     "     " | 36 50 |
|---|---|---|
| Mar. 6. | "     "     " | 63 66 |
| April 6. | "     "     " | 12 08 |
| June 7. | "     "     " | 29 21 |
| Oct. 11. | "     "     " | 35 91 |
| Nov. 11. | "     "     " | 20 32 |
| Dec. 8. | "     "     " | 17 82 |

1872.

| Jan. 10. | "     "     " | 30 14 |
|---|---|---|
| Feb. 10. | "     "     " | 108 33 |
| Mar. 15. | "     "     " | 133 32 |
| April 11. | "     "     " | 53 08 |

| Total | $1,001 12 |
|---|---|

1870. *John Bunce.*

| May 9. | Hardware | $95 40 |
|---|---|---|
| June 22. | " | 41 95 |
| Aug. 13. | " | 29 74 |
| Nov. 18. | " | 79 86 |
| Dec. 12. | " | 28 42 |

1871.

| Jan. 6. | " | 45 52 |
|---|---|---|
| Feb. 17. | " | 21 25 |
| Mar. 6. | " | 12 52 |

| Carried forward | $354 46 |
|---|---|

| | | | |
|---|---|---|---:|
| | Brought forward | | $354 46 |
| April | 5.—Hardware | | 16 66 |
| May | 11. | " | 24 92 |
| Aug. | 10. | " | 30 45 |
| Sept. | 14. | " | 12 77 |
| Oct. | 11. | " | 19 96 |
| Nov. | 10. | " | 16 20 |
| Dec. | 11. | " | 40 15 |

1872.

| | | | |
|---|---|---|---:|
| Jan. | 10. | " | 64 23 |
| Mar. | 12. | " | 51 00 |
| April 10. | | " | 20 42 |

Total................................. $651 42

1870.                    *Jos. H. Mumby.*

| | | | |
|---|---|---|---:|
| July | 9.—Horse feed | | $44 32 |
| Aug. | 23. | " | 23 14 |
| Sept. | 9. | " | 23 13 |
| Oct. | 10. | " | 13 29 |
| Nov. | 10. | " | 32 70 |
| Dec. | 8. | " | 17 87 |

1871.

| | | | |
|---|---|---|---:|
| Jan. | 5. | " | 21 21 |
| Mar. | 7. | " | 16 99 |
| April | 8. | " | 19 08 |
| June | 6. | " | 19 19 |
| July | 12. | " | 24 10 |
| Aug. | 9. | " | 16 27 |
| Oct. | 9. | " | 49 41 |
| Nov. | 8. | " | 19 70 |
| Dec. | 11. | " | 20 05 |

1872.

| | | | |
|---|---|---|---:|
| Jan. | 11. | " | 47 12 |
| Feb. | 10. | " | 25 80 |
| Mar. | 12. | " | 18 88 |
| April | 9. | " | 17 20 |

Total................................. $469 45

1870.                    *Wm. Taylor & Sons.*

| | |
|---|---:|
| May   9.—Pipe, washers, etc. | $24 86 |

1871.

| | |
|---|---:|
| Mar.   11.—Iron and labor | 111 65 |
| Dec.   5.        " | 404 85 |

Carried forward........................ $541 36

Brought forward ......................... $541 36
1872.

Jan. 11.—Iron-work........................... 56 30
Feb. 12.    "    ............................. 81 20

Total..................................... $678 86

1870.            *New York Oxygen Gas Co.*

July  6.—Oxygen gas......................... $329 20
Aug.  9.    "    ............................. 1,270 98
Sept. 7.    "    .............................. 658 36
Oct.  3.    "    .............................. 753 82
Nov.  7.    "    .............................. 668 99
Dec.  5.    "    .............................. 543 35

1871.

Jan.  5.    "    .............................. 297 85
Feb.  9.    "    .............................. 159 99

Total........... ........................... $4,682 54

1870.            *Jas. McFarlan, Jr.*

Feb.  7.—Iron-work........................... $78 84
Mar.  8.    "    ............................. 103 50
June  6.    "    ............................. 61 42
Sept. 7.—Labor, etc......................... 19 26
Nov.  8.—Iron-work, labor, etc................. 68 47
Dec.  6.    "        "    .................... 20 82

1871.

April 4.—Cylinders, etc........................ 64 84
Aug.  8.—Iron-work............................ 11 00

1872.

Feb.  6.    "    ............................. 44 40

Total..................................... $472 55

1870.            *Hazard Powder Co.*

Mar. 10.—Powder............................ $600 00
April 13.   "    ............................ 1,100 00
May  3.    "    ............................. 825 00
Nov. 16.   "    ............................. 11 00

Total..................................... $2,536 00

1870.            *I. E. White.*

Mar. 10.—Piles and labor..................... $221 80
July  5.—Piles, bolts, etc..................... 688 37

Carried forward ......................... $910 17

|  | Brought forward | $910 17 |
|---|---|---|
| Sept. | 7.—Piles and labor | 60 75 |
| Oct. | 4.        " | 406 63 |
| Nov. | 9.        " | 210 10 |

1871.

| Mar. | 10.—Use of pile-driver | 60 00 |
|---|---|---|

|  | Total | $1,647 65 |
|---|---|---|

1870.                    *Abbott & Co.*

| April | 5.—Gravel roofing | $147 00 |
|---|---|---|
| July | 7.        " | 17 80 |
| Aug. | 11.        " | 41 40 |
| Sept. | 7.        " | 21 25 |
| Dec. | 12.—Cementing boilers | 16 20 |

|  | Total | $243 65 |
|---|---|---|

1870.                    *B. T. Benton.*

| June | 6.—Iron pipes and labor | $173 75 |
|---|---|---|
| July | 12.        "        " | 401 94 |
| Aug. | 10.—Steam pipes and fittings | 347 95 |
| Oct. | 5.—Iron pipes and fittings | 357 51 |
| Nov. | 8.        "        " | 117 09 |
| Dec. | 7.        "        " | 125 97 |

1871.

| Feb. | 15.        "        " | 105 10 |
|---|---|---|

|  | Total | $1,629 31 |
|---|---|---|

1870.                    *Davis & Riker.*

| June | 22.—Pipe, fittings, etc | $38 94 |
|---|---|---|
| Oct. | 10.—Packing, copper, etc | 7 25 |
| Nov. | 8.—Packing, brass, etc | 32 15 |

1871.

| Nov. | 9.—Spikes | 6 75 |
|---|---|---|

1872.

| Mar. | 30.        " | 7 00 |
|---|---|---|
| April | 30.        " | 7 00 |

|  | Total | $99 09 |
|---|---|---|

1870.                    *John Frazier.*

| Mar. | 8.—Powder cans | $175 40 |
|---|---|---|
| April | 5.        " | 125 50 |

|  | Carried forward | $300 90 |
|---|---|---|

|  | Brought forward | $300 90 |
|---|---|---|
| May | 7.—Powder cans | 45 28 |
| June | 8.—Iron and tin work | 47 75 |
| July | 6.      " | 21 65 |
| Oct. | 7.      " | 23 51 |
| Nov. | 11.      " | 11 90 |
| Dec. | 14.      " | 20 15 |
| Sept. | 10.      " | 11 20 |

|  | Total | $482 34 |
|---|---|---|

1870.                    *Laflin & Rand Powder Co.*

| Mar. 10.—Powder | $45 00 |
|---|---|

1870.                    *Holton & Gray.*

| Jan. | 3.—Rubber washers and springs | $424 87 |
|---|---|---|
| " | 10.—Rubber gaskets | 70 69 |
| April | 5.      " | 59 25 |

1871.                    *Holton & Dickinson.*

| Feb. | 18.—Rubber gaskets and washers | 76 31 |
|---|---|---|
| May | 11.      "       " | 37 13 |

|  | Total | $668 25 |
|---|---|---|

1870.                    *Henry Elliott & Co.*

| June | 20.—Rubber boots | $321 48 |
|---|---|---|
| July | 7.      " | 288 00 |
| Aug. | 16.      " | 898 85 |
| Sept. | 23.      " | 100 78 |
| Nov. | 18.      " | 90 67 |
| Dec. | 21.      " | 549 07 |

1871.

| Aug. | 10.      " | 59 40 |
|---|---|---|

1871.                    *Wallace & Elliott.*

| Aug. | 10.—Rubber boots | 22 67 |
|---|---|---|
| Sept. | 12.      " | 44 70 |

1872.

| Jan. | 18.      " | 12 63 |
|---|---|---|

|  | Total | $2,388 25 |
|---|---|---|

1870.                    *Powell Manufacturing Co.*

| Mar. | 8.—Powder cans | $128 95 |
|---|---|---|
| Oct. | 4.—Lead and labor | 23 00 |

|  | Carried forward | $151 95 |
|---|---|---|

|  | | |
|---|---:|---:|
| Brought forward...................... | $151 | 95 |

**1871.**

| Jan. 5.—Tin and labor...................... | 227 | 50 |

**1872.** *R. I. Powell & Co.*

| Feb. 28.—Repairing pumps...................... | 2 | 50 |
| Total...................... | $381 | 95 |

**1870.** *Cuthbert & Cunningham.*

| Mar. 10.—Coal tar...................... | $17 | 75 |

**1870.**

| Oct. 26.—W. C. Kingsley, superintendent......... | $50,000 | 00 |
| Nov. 10.  "        "        ......... | 75,000 | 00 |
| Total...................... | $125,000 | 00 |

**1870.** *C. & R. Poillon.*

| Mar. 9.—Spars............................... | $25 | 50 |
| Aug. 9.   "   ............................... | 103 | 00 |

**1871.**

| Jan. 6.   "   ............................... | 34 | 00 |
| Total...................... | $167 | 50 |

**1870.** *S. S. Goodwin.*

| Mar. 9.—Earth filling...................... | $82 | 00 |

**1871.** *W. S. Tisdale & Co.*

| Sept. 12.—Nails and spikes...................... | $17 | 50 |
| Nov. 21.    "        ...................... | 82 | 00 |

**1872.**

| Jan. 18.   "   ............................... | 43 | 10 |
| Feb. 13.   "   ............................... | 210 | 75 |
| Mar. 14.   "   ............................... | 81 | 75 |
| April 9.   "   ............................... | 25 | 75 |
| Total...................... | $460 | 85 |

**1870.**

| Mar. 14.—Miscellaneous items from petty cash..... | $24 | 99 |
| April 5.    "          "          "    ..... | 53 | 15 |
| May 5.    "          "          "    ..... | 65 | 82 |
| "   31.    "          "          "    ..... | 73 | 91 |
| June 30.    "          "          "    ..... | 59 | 94 |
| Carried forward ...................... | $277 | 84 |

8

|  |  | Brought forward | $277 84 |
|---|---|---|---|
| July | 30.—Miscellaneous items from petty cash | | 18 10 |
| Aug. | 31. | " " " | 87 30 |
| Sept. | 30. | " " " | 30 52 |
| Oct. | 31. | " " " | 1 00 |
| Nov. | 30. | " " " | 36 89 |
| Dec. | 31. | " " " | 56 00 |

1871.

| Jan. | 31. | " " " | 37 83 |
|---|---|---|---|
| Feb. | 28. | " " " | 86 30 |
| Mar. | 31. | " " " | 59 55 |
| April | 29. | " " " | 32 87 |
| May | 31. | " " " | 82 24 |
| June | 3. | " " " | 77 90 |
| July | 31. | " " " | 79 07 |
| Aug. | 31. | " " " | 8 83 |
| Sept. | 30. | " " " | 40 18 |
| Oct. | 31. | " " " | 28 00 |
| Nov. | 29. | " " " | 110 44 |
| Dec. | 30. | " " " | 40 39 |

1872.

| Jan. | 31. | " " " | 125 23 |
|---|---|---|---|
| Feb. | 29. | " " " | 59 38 |
| Mar. | 30. | " " " | 38 94 |
| April | 30. | " " " | 1 75 |

| Total | $1,416 55 |
|---|---|

*Miscellaneous Items.*

1870.

| April | 4.—W. H. Paine, labor and material at caisson. | $70 82 |
|---|---|---|
| " | 9.—N. Morton, coal tar | 24 00 |
| " | 11.—A. K. Meserole, coal, lime and cement | 31 75 |
| " | 13.—India Rubber Roofing Company, roofing sheds | 125 91 |
| May | 2.—John McRoberts, gravel and sand | 171 35 |
| " | 3.—R. J. Hutchinson, powder canisters | 75 00 |
| | P. Bracken, stone and sand | 72 00 |
| | Rubber Roofing Company, roofing | 23 16 |
| " | 4.—J. A. Bouker, stone | 486 28 |
| " | 5.—J. S. Turner, water | 21 00 |
| | Tillotson & Co., blasting wire | 60 00 |
| " | 9.—John J. Wilson, cement | 214 00 |
| " | 11.—W. M. Tebo, towing mud scows, timber, dredge, etc | 1,562 50 |
| " | 13.—I. Woodbury, fuse | 66 00 |
| | F. Hobson & Son, steel | 42 17 |
| " | 18.—John Maginn, services launching and towing caisson | 110 00 |

| Carried forward | $3,155 94 |
|---|---|

| | | |
|---|---|---|
| Brought forward | $3,155 | 94 |
| April 23.—Wharfage on caisson | 176 | 00 |
| " 19.—P. C. Shultz, towing caisson | 408 | 00 |
| June 7.—Cement | 1 | 80 |
| " 18.—P. C. Coffin, spikes, nails and steel | 75 | 56 |
| " 6.—J. S. Turner, water | 79 | 50 |
| John Bowie, lead castings | 28 | 50 |
| " 9.—Wm. Dorrian, rigging used at launching caisson | 249 | 15 |
| " 11.—Vanpelt & Moore, canvas | 48 | 80 |
| Armstrong & Blacklin, gas pipes and fittings | 924 | 97 |
| " 14.—J. T. Martin, inspector of dredging | 234 | 00 |
| " 20.—C. N. Flanders, oil and cans | 88 | 26 |
| Brien, Adams & Brien, plumbing-work | 162 | 42 |
| " 25.—A. M. C. Smith, belting | 26 | 46 |
| July 6.—Lindsay, Walton & Co., spikes, sponges, etc | 40 | 24 |
| Aug. 9.—Lindsay, Walton & Co., felting boiler | 25 | 00 |
| Sept. 7. " spikes | | 90 |
| Oct. 8.—Walton & Co., sponges, etc | 9 | 82 |
| July 8.—American Tool Steel Company, steel | 170 | 31 |
| Aug. 11. " " " | 20 | 55 |
| Sept. 23. " " " | 32 | 98 |
| Oct. 7. " " " | 113 | 23 |
| Nov. 10. " " " | 82 | 21 |
| Dec. 5. " " " | 71 | 27 |
| July 29.—Francis Hobson & Son, steel | 133 | 73 |
| Aug. 26. " " | 24 | 65 |
| July 6.—F. H. Schnider & Co., cementing boiler | 39 | 00 |
| " 7.—P. C. Schultz, towing scows | 42 | 00 |
| " 12.—G. R. Alexander, H. W. lumber | 108 | 92 |
| " 15.—A. M. C. Smith, hose | 136 | 00 |
| " 18.—C. N. Flanders, oil | 64 | 80 |
| " 30.—Mulford & Co., nails and spikes | 17 | 00 |
| New Jersey Car Spring Company, gaskets | 19 | 97 |
| Aug. 11.—Vanpelt & Moore, canvas, rope, oil clothing, etc | 477 | 13 |
| Sept. 10.—Vanpelt & Moore, canvas, rope, oil clothing | 144 | 83 |
| Oct. 21. " canvas and rope | 158 | 46 |
| Dec. 10. " oil clothing | 118 | 36 |
| | | |
| 1871. | | |
| Jan. 19.—Vanpelt & Moore, gunny bags, etc | 13 | 30 |
| Mar. 8. " " | 11 | 00 |
| | | |
| 1870. | | |
| Aug. 10.—W. C. Bramhill & Co., belting, packing, etc | 25 | 95 |
| Engel, Rothermel & Co., coal | 632 | 70 |
| " 11.—C. N. Flanders, oil | 72 | 50 |
| Richard Bracken, stone | 66 | 50 |
| | | |
| Carried forward | $8,532 | 67 |

| | | |
|---|---|---|
| Brought forward .......................... | $8,532 | 67 |
| Aug. 11.—Armstrong & Blacklin, plumbing and gas | | |
| pipes, etc......................... | 400 | 32 |
| " 13.—G. L. Enggren, boring at Pier 29........ | 664 | 01 |
| " 15.—Caffrey & Wilson, testing cylinders, etc.. | 86 | 55 |
| " 16.—G. L. Enggren, boring at Pier 29......... | 286 | 00 |
| " 31.—John Voorhies, stone.................... | 96 | 25 |
| Sept. 1.—Geo. Carr & Co., felting boilers......... | 249 | 00 |
| " 7.—P. W. Shute, slate...................... | 12 | 00 |
| " 10.—C. N. Flanders, oils.................... | 268 | 30 |
| Oct. 4.—Union Ackron Cement Company, cement. | 37 | 00 |
| " 7.—S. T. Baker & Co., oil.................. | 112 | 80 |
| Nov. 10.        "             " .................... | 55 | 63 |
| 1871. | | |
| Jan. 9.        "             " .................. | 59 | 25 |
| 1870. | | |
| Oct. 26.—R. Dudgeon, repairing jacks............ | 48 | 50 |
| " 10.—C. N. Flanders, oil................... | 63 | 80 |
| " 18.—J. J. Reimer & Co., wooden-ware........ | 42 | 02 |
| M. McKinney, iron-work............... | 26 | 40 |
| Chapman Slate Company, slate......... | 30 | 00 |
| " 26.—Smith & Hall, rollers, wedges, etc....... | 23 | 87 |
| Nov. 18.   .   "             " ........ | 11 | 91 |
| Dec. 12.        "             " ........ | 74 | 72 |
| 1871. | | |
| May 12.        "             " ........ | 19 | 20 |
| 1872. | | |
| Jan. 8.        "             " ........ | 65 | 80 |
| Mar. 13.        "             " ........ | 48 | 00 |
| 1870. | | |
| Nov. 8.—Phelps & Kimpland, piles, towing, etc... | 743 | 36 |
| 1871. | | |
| Feb. 16.        "             "       ... | 308 | 00 |
| July · 10.        "        storage on timber... | 57 | 90 |
| 1870. | | |
| Nov. 8.—Marriott McKinney, spikes, lewises, etc... | 150 | 80 |
| " 10.—Armstrong & Blacklin, plumbing and gas- | | |
| fitting........................... | 119 | 61 |
| Dec. 7.—Armstrong & Blacklin, plumbing and gas- | | |
| fitting........................... | 171 | 83 |
| 1871. | | |
| Jan. 6.—Armstrong & Blacklin, plumbing and gas- | | |
| fitting........................... | 61 | 97 |
| 1870. | | |
| May 31.—Bangs & Gaynor, cement.............. | 62 | 27 |
| Carried forward .......................... | $12,989 | 74 |

| | | | | |
|---|---|---|---|---|
| | Brought forward .......................... | | $12,989 | 74 |
| Nov. | 8.—Bangs & Gaynor, cement................ | | 81 | 88 |

1871.

| | | | | | |
|---|---|---|---|---|---|
| May | 31. | " | freight................ | 34 | 25 |
| June | 6. | " | cement................ | 112 | 00 |

1870.

| | | | | | |
|---|---|---|---|---|---|
| Nov. | 11.—C. N. Flanders, oil..................... | | | 122 | 18 |
| Dec. | 13. | " | " ..................... | 90 | 80 |

1871.

| | | | | | |
|---|---|---|---|---|---|
| Jan. | 12. | " | " ..................... | 82 | 20 |
| Mar. | 10. | " | " ..................... | 61 | 00 |
| May | 31. | " | " ..................... | 9 | 80 |
| June | 9. | " | " ..................... | 61 | 80 |
| Aug. | 12. | " | " ..................... | 12 | 00 |
| Oct. | 10. | " | " ..................... | 73 | 40 |

1870.

| | | | | | |
|---|---|---|---|---|---|
| Nov. | 18.—G. W. Gallaway, oil.................... | | | 54 | 25 |
| Dec. | 8. | " | " ..................... | 44 | 00 |
| Nov. | 18.—C. H. Delamater, iron-work............ | | | 91 | 95 |
| Dec. | 7. | " | " .......... | 128 | 73 |

1872.

| | | | | | |
|---|---|---|---|---|---|
| April | 24. | " | " .......... | 62 | 18 |

1870.

| | | | | |
|---|---|---|---|---|
| Nov. | 8.—N. & H. O'Donnell, molasses hogsheads.. | | 13 | 00 |
| | H. A. Rogers & Co., felting boilers...... | | 191 | 70 |
| " | 9.—Forge Company, canopy for forge....... | | 14 | 50 |
| " | 10.—D. Fithian, window sashes............. | | 11 | 50 |
| Dec. | 6.—W. C. Wright & Co., oil.............. | | 157 | 95 |
| " | 8.—F. W. Devoe, oil...................... | | 28 | 60 |

1871.

| | | | | | |
|---|---|---|---|---|---|
| Feb. | 17. | " | " ..................... | 23 | 59 |
| Mar. | 8. | " | " ..................... | 47 | 97 |
| May | 11. | " | " ..................... | 154 | 32 |
| July | 19. | " | " ..................... | 100 | 17 |
| Oct. | 10. | " | " ..................... | 61 | 17 |

1870.

| | | | | |
|---|---|---|---|---|
| Dec. | 7.—Joseph Nason & Co., pipes and fittings... | | 340 | 78 |

1871.

| | | | | | |
|---|---|---|---|---|---|
| Jan. | 19. | " | " ... | 70 | 74 |

1870.

| | | | | |
|---|---|---|---|---|
| Dec. | 15.—Jas. S. Turner, water................. | | 20 | 20 |

1871.

| | | | | | |
|---|---|---|---|---|---|
| June | 6. | " | " ................. | 119 | 25 |

| | | | | |
|---|---|---|---|---|
| | Carried forward .......................... | | $15,467 | 60 |

Brought forward.......................... $15,467 60

1870.

Dec. 16.—Salamander Works, pipe and fitting.....   34 80
"   23.—Chrome Steel Company, steel............   5 27

1871.

Mar. 8.          "            "   ............  15 98

1870.

Dec. 21.—Chapman Slate Company, slate..........  30 00

1871.

July 14.          "            "   ..........  30 50

1870.

Dec. 12.—Jas. Cumings, labor and material........  72 00
        "            "        ........  32 75
        "            "        ........  43 75

1872.

Mar. 14.—Jas. Cumings, blocks and fittings........  53 75
Dec.  8.—H. A. Rogers & Co., belting, etc........  10 30

1871.

Jan.  5.—D. Fithian, window sashes..............  26 50
Mar.  8.—W. E. Woodruff, painting..............  151 20
April 8.—D. Fithian, window sashes..............  14 70
"   11.—W. E. Woodruff, painting..............  199 90
Jan. 12.—J. J. Reimer & Co., wooden-ware........  44 01
"    4.—Salamander Grate Bar Co., grate bars....  133 12
June 17.      "       "       "       "    ....  79 30
Nov. 21.      "       "       "       "    ....  112 71

1872.

Mar. 25.      "       "       "       "    ....  26 81

1871.

Feb.  7.—Washington Iron-Works, iron and labor.  129 11
Mar.  8.—Livingston & Cherritree Manufacturing
            Company, files.....................  14 98
"   14.—Eckford Iron-Works, iron..............  12 32
April 4.—David Dows & Co., storage on cement...  378 43
"    6.—Page, Kidder & Fletcher, coal tar and
            pitch......................  26 25
May 13.—Page, Kidder & Fletcher, coal tar and
            pitch......................  71 25
"   10.—Buell & Co., gravel....................  23 59
Oct. 12.      "    roofing....................  52 02
Dec.  5.      "        "   ....................  447 34

1872.

Jan. 11.      "        "   ....................  39 21
Feb.  7.      "        "   ....................  22 50
                                              ——————
Carried forward .......................... $17,801 95

|  |  |  |
|---|---|---|
| Brought forward .......................... | | $17,801 95 |

1871.

May 9.—New York Creosoting Works, creosoting
plank .............................. 600 00
June 6.—New York Creosoting Works, creosoting
plank .............................. 344 48
Sept. 8.—New York Creosoting Works, creosoting
plank .............................. 162 40
May 9.—W. L. Holmes, horse feed.............. 25 56
" 8.—W. H. Rushmore, cement.............. 100 00
April 6.—Henry Moore, oil cups, etc.............. 44 00
" 19.—A. H. Acken, traveling expenses........ 36 73
June 12. " " ........ 61 67
July 10. " " ........ 36 81
May 8.—Mason & Martin, repairing boiler........ 130 00
Nov. 11. " " 120 13
June 8.—Wm. Corchrane, labor as rigger........ 113 17
Union Chemical Works, tar............ 45 00
Aug. 14. " tar, pitch and felt 75 33

1872.

Jan. 15. " " " 204 33
Feb. 7. " " " 56 00
Mar. 28. " " " 56 00
April 30. " " " 9 83

1871.

June 6.—N. & H. O'Donnell, hogsheads.......... 48 00
" 5.—Jas. Goff, use of small boats at launch... 40 00
W. E. Woodruff, painting............. 258 83
Sept. 14. " " ............. 41 62
June 8.—W. H. Webb, wharfage of caisson and one
barrel of pitch..................... 93 50
" 14.—Delaware & Hudson Canal Co., coal..... 17 00
July 21. " " " ..... 195 50
June 23.—John Marx, galvanizing iron............. 20 52
Sept. 14. " " ............ 30 54
Dec. 15. " " ............ 20 64

1872.

April 16. " " ............ 87 90

1871.

June 8.—John McGinn, services at launching caisson 50 00
July 14.—Brien, Adams & Brien, plumbing-work... 110 45
" 10.—Geo. Brown, wharfage of caisson........ 90 00
" 12.—T. J. Meadon, tinning on caisson........ 108 50
C. Donohue, horse-shoeing............. 15 37

1872.

Jan. 6. " " ............. 15 00
April 30. " " ............. 12 00

Carried forward ...................... $21,278 76

| | | |
|---|---|---|
| Brought forward........................ | $21,278 76 | |

**1871.**

| | | |
|---|---|---|
| July 19.—John Gray & Co., woodenware......... | 15 50 | |
| Aug. 10.      "              "       .......... | 12 50 | |
| Dec. 12.      "              "       .......... | 22 75 | |

**1872.**

| | | |
|---|---|---|
| Feb. 13.      "              "       .......... | 22 50 | |
| Mar. 14.      "              "       .......... | 32 50 | |
| April 9.      "              "       .......... | 32 50 | |

**1871.**

| | | |
|---|---|---|
| July 10.—R. I. Powell, tinware.................. | 17 25 | |
| "     19.—Rubber suit for inspector............. | 15 00 | |
| "     19.—Repairs to diving-bell................. | 8 00 | |
| Aug. 14.—A. C. Keeney, sand.................... | 462 82 | |
| Nov. 11.      "              "      ............... | 152 57 | |
| Aug. 10.—W. A. Freeborn & Co., asphalt, tar, mops, | | |
| etc............................. | 99 88 | |
| "     21.—E. K. Richards & Co., ship timber, knees, | 12 00 | |
| Sept. 11.—Union White Lead Co., white and red lead | 71 75 | |
| Nov. 21.      "              oil and lead..... | 53 00 | |
| Sept. 12.—Page, Thomas & Co., roofing... ....... | 40 23 | |
| "      8.—A. M. Ingersoll, boat and oars.......... | 80 00 | |
| "      8.—E. Daly, adm'x, repairing wagon........ | 15 00 | |
| Horse-keeping for 15 months, 1 horse.... | 375 00 | |
| "     23.—John Burt, diving at Pier 29............ | 150 00 | |
| Oct. 12.—Nicholas Kane, use of tarpaulin........ | 6 50 | |
| Dec. 12.      "       chain, canvas, etc....... | 45 05 | |

**1872.**

| | | |
|---|---|---|
| Mar. 14.      "       hammocks............. | 84 62 | |

**1871.**

| | | |
|---|---|---|
| Oct. 10.—Morris & Cumings, excavating and re- | | |
| moving crib at Pier 29............. | 9,000 00 | |

**1872.**

| | | |
|---|---|---|
| April 11.—Taking up stone from the river at R. H.... | 250 00 | |

**1871.**

| | | |
|---|---|---|
| Oct. 11.—Richardson, Meriam & Co, drum stand | | |
| and grate........................,..... | 18 75 | |

**1872.**

| | | |
|---|---|---|
| Mar. 11.—Richardson, Meriam & Co., spur wheel... | 30 00 | |
| April 9.      "          "      castings and straps | 16 28 | |

**1871.**

| | | |
|---|---|---|
| Oct. 12.—Atlantic Dock Co., wharfage of caisson.. | 936 00 | |
| "     23.—W. D. Andrews & Bro., use of engine and | | |
| pump..... ...................... | 236 25 | |
| Nov. 15.—James L. Moore, repairing harness, etc... | 15 00 | |

| | | |
|---|---|---|
| Carried forward ........................ | $33,607 96 | |

| | |
|---|---:|
| Brought forward . . . . . . . . . . . . . . . | $33,607 96 |

**1872.**
April 30.—James L. Moore, repairing harness, etc. . | 12 44

**1871.**
Nov. 11.—Cory & Co., oil . . . . . . . . . . . . . . . . . . . . . . | 98 83
Dec. 12.        "       " . . . . . . . . . . . . . . . . . . . . . . | 43 35

**1872.**
Feb. 5.     "       " . . . . . . . . . . . . . . . . . . . | 84 15
Mar. 11.     "       " . . . . . . . . . . . . . . . . . . | 78 30
April 8.     "       " . . . . . . . . . . . . . . . . . . . | 170 55

**1871.**
Nov. 10.—John Cochrane, agent, iron-work . . . . . . . . | 13 20
Dec. 5.      "     "      " . . . . . . . . . | 603 50

**1872.**
Mar. 11.      "      "      " . . . . . . . . . | 24 00
April 8.      "      "      " . . . . . . . . . | 55 80

**1871.**
Nov. 6.—Pechell & Co., paint . . . . . . . . . . . . . . . . . . | 84 82
           Wm. Butcher Steel Works, steel links, and
               pins . . . . . . . . . . . . . . . . . . . . . . . . . | 1,109 68
**1872.**
April 16.—Wm. Butcher Steel Works, steel forgings
               and pins . . . . . . . . . . . . . . . . . . . . . . | 4,903 73

**1871.**
Nov. 6.—McMann & Russell, iron pipe fittings . . . . | 310 36
Dec. 4.—R. A. Chesebrough, oil . . . . . . . . . . . . . . . | 55 50

**1872.**
Feb. 7.     "        " . . . . . . . . . . . . . . . . . | 26 70
Mar. 25.     "        " . . . . . . . . . . . . . . . . . | 38 92

**1871.**
Dec. 5.—S. S. Goodwin, earth filling . . . . . . . . . . . . | 138 80
Dec. 4.—B. J. Drew, stoves and fixtures . . . . . . . . . | 49 85

**1872.**
Jan. 6.     "        "        " . . . . . . . . . . | 46 62
Feb. 5.     "        "        " . . . . . . . . . . | 46 28
Mar. 11.     "        "        " . . . . . . . . . . | 28 20

**1871.**
Dec. 4.—Asbestos Felting Co., covering boilers . . . . | 830 65

**1872.**
Jan. 9.      "         "     . . . . . | 15 75
Feb. 6.      "         "     . . . . . | 77 75

| | |
|---|---:|
| Carried forward . . . . . . . . . . . . . . . . . . . . . . . . . . | $42,555 69 |

| | | | |
|---|---|---|---|
| Brought forward | | $42,555 | 69 |

1871.

Dec. 13.—T. & A. Walsh, dock stone ............... 826 56

1872.

| Jan. | 13. | " | " | ............... | 522 | 50 |
|---|---|---|---|---|---|---|
| Feb. | 8. | " | " | ............... | 375 | 00 |
| Mar. | 19. | " . | " | ............... | 176 | 25 |
| April | 12. | " | " | ............... | 217 | 50 |

1871.

Dec. 8.—Chas. A. Willard, coal ................. 25 75

1872.

Feb. 28.      "      " ................. 7 00

Theo. Smith & Bro., rebuilding buckets
(dredge), and for repairs and alterations,    1,355 78

1871.

Dec. 12.—Clark, Wilson & Co., hardware .......... 20 89

1872.

| Jan. | 20. | " | " | ........... | 13 | 37 |
|---|---|---|---|---|---|---|
| " | 9.—Hess & Co., galvanizing iron ........... | | | | 134 | 28 |
| | T. New, roofing ...................... | | | | 169 | 24 |
| " | 10.—Leeds, Clark & Co., oiled clothing ....... | | | | 228 | 00 |
| " | 11.—D. Fithian, window sashes ............. | | | | 91 | 20 |
| Feb. | 8. " " ............. | | | | 36 | 00 |
| Jan. | 18.—Ash & Buckbee, gas-fittings .......... | | | | 18 | 37 |
| Feb. | 13. " plumbing-work ........ | | | | 19 | 01 |
| Jan. | 18.—H. A. White Company, oil ............. | | | | 15 | 50 |
| Feb. | 13. " " " ............. | | | | 15 | 50 |
| Jan. | 17.—T. A. Scott, diving ....... | | | | 357 | 50 |
| " | 15.—Goodyear Rubber Company, rubber boots | | | | 809 | 55 |
| Feb. | 10. " " | | | | 894 | 80 |
| " | 5.—Pitkin & Co., bedding ............... | | | | 67 | 80 |
| | Caffrey & Wilson, hydrogen gas ........ | | | | 67 | 27 |
| " | 6.—Matthew March, leather ............... | | | | 11 | 36 |
| " | 10.—A. Schraeder, cylinder, bed-plate, etc .... | | | | 83 | 42 |
| April | 30. " hose pipes ............... | | | | 10 | 00 |
| Feb. | 13.—G. A. Merwin & Co., coffee ............. | | | | 30 | 00 |
| Mar. | 25. " " ............. | | | | 25 | 65 |
| April | 9. " " ............. | | | | 27 | 81 |
| Feb. | 13.—J. W. Kissam, tin-ware ............... | | | | 11 | 35 |
| Mar. | 14. " cook utensils, tin-ware, etc | | | | 24 | 75 |
| Feb. | 13.—West Virginia Oil & Oil Land Company, oil ..................................... | | | | 44 | 50 |
| Mar. | 14.—West Virginia Oil & Oil Land Company, oil ..................................... | | | | 45 | 75 |
| April | 9.—West Virginia Oil & Oil Land Company, oil ..................................... | | | | 90 | 25 |
| Feb. | 13.—Morris, Tasker & Co., iron cocks ........ | | | | 140 | 00 |

| | | | |
|---|---|---|---|
| Carried forward | | $49,565 | 15 |

|  | Brought forward.......................... | $49,565 15 |
| Feb. | 13.—Howard & Morse, wire-work........... | 23 55 |
| " | 10.—M. Murphy, pilotage of caisson........ | 150 00 |
| Mar. | 14.—Wm. Porter & Sons, lamps, etc......... | 105 47 |
|  | G. Tagliabue, glass tubes.............. | 10 20 |
| " | 13.—Geo. T. Sutton & Co., sugar............ | 54 51 |
| April 10. | "          "          ............. | 52 25 |
| Mar. | 13.—Pearce & Mitchell, castings........... | 21 45 |
| " | 11.—Building Material Co., cement.......... | 2,100 00 |
| " | 12.—N. Y. Gas-Light Co., gas and fixtures.... | 853 48 |
| April | 8.—Jas. Williamson & Co., pig iron........ | 1,150 00 |
|  | Jas. O'Brien, ballast stone ............. | 335 00 |
|  | Chas. McManus, gravel ................. | 346 37 |
| " | 9.—Phœnix Iron Co., eye bars and pins..... | 156 42 |
|  | Phelps, Dodge & Co., pig-lead.......... | 3,713 21 |
|  | N. Y. Lighterage Co., lightering pig iron. | 18 75 |
| " | 12.—Martin J. Brien, plumbing............. | 20 13 |
| " | 10.—N. Y. Gas-Light Co., gas.............. | 369 90 |

$59,045 84

Less amount received from Wilder
Son & Co., for labor..........$219 25
Less discount from Egleston Bros. &
Co.... ....................... 80 81
————
300 06

Total............................. ....... $58,745 78

Total expenditures on account of the bridge and its
appurtenances, to May 1, 1872.................. $2,657,389 49
Paid for New York City bonds................... 248,000 00

Total payments............................. $2,905,389 49.

JOHN H. PRENTICE, *Treasurer*,
O. P. QUINTARD, *Secretary*.